A Bite-Si

Three Short Stories

Messages

The Gospel of Vic the Fish

The Theatre of Ghosts

Victor Hill

Published by Bite-Sized Books Ltd 2019

Bite-Sized Books Ltd, Cleeve Road, Goring RG8 9BJ UK
information@bite-sizedbooks.com
Registered in the UK. Company Registration No: 9395379
ISBN: 9781098530822

CONTENTS

Messages

I simply cannot believe this child. Angelica is a nightmare. This morning she went off to school with the key to my wine chiller. I was deprived of a few glasses of eagerly anticipated chilled Mersault with my lunch.

Ping. A message from Belinda: *Belinda called but was unable to leave a message.*

A double whammy. Belinda has disappeared to America on business. And Varina has sped off to an "ashram" in India, leaving young Angelica here in my care. Both think they shall be absent for "at least" three weeks.

Jack has turned churlish. Yes, I have sired a churl. And the girl-child is making him worse. He used to be such a delightful little boy. Fourteen: what a repulsive age. And it can only get worse. How the fuck am I supposed to write a novel, with only Anca the maid and Pavel the gardener to help here? It's ridiculous. Pavel is not even a proper gardener but a twenty-seven year-old dancer by trade, if you please.

I should explain that, Belinda, my wife (we tied the knot one long hot summer in Paris) is a hot-shot city lawyer. She earns more in one month than I have earned from writing in the last ten years. That sleek German machine in the gravel drive outside was a Christmas present. We certainly couldn't live in this lovely old rectory-with-oasthouse on my precarious earnings. But she does travel a lot.

Did you say you enjoy crime fiction? Can I interest you in *medieval crime fiction*? You may have heard of me. Leonard Norman? *Murder at the Abbey*? *The Pope Must*

Die? *Altars of Blood*? Just a few of my titles. No? They're all set in the middle ages, often in monasteries, usually in my native Kent. Ken Follett might have teams of researchers but at least I have the internet. Plus I spend a lot of time in churchyards. Or, in extremis, there is Maidstone library.

I've just read a message from Simon, my agent at *Heinrich & Steadman*. He says they ran my latest plotline for *Enter the Stranger* on a focus group composed of their "target demographic" (whatever that is) and the consensus was that the whole thing is *too sepia*. They want more realistic violence – even gore. Simon thinks there should be less narrative and more psychopaths.

Well, they can have gore if they like. I'll give them gore: brains splattered on flagstones; peasants crushed by falling cathedral masonry; priests having their eyes gouged out…Come to think of it the mysterious stranger who appears in the village of Trosley could turn out to be a psychopath – that's really rather a good idea. Well done, Si. One by one the children go missing – but no one can pin anything on him.

I can hear the conversation at WH Smith, Gatwick, even now. *Is that the new Leonard Norman?   Oh yes, it's gripping. He's very dark, isn't he…?*

A text message from Belinda: *Busy, busy, busy xxx.*

It's not even as if we are close friends with Varina. I seem to remember we first met her at that meditation class last year. She made a rather sinister impression on me. She told me I was bearing the burden of a terrible crime that I had committed in a previous life. I mean, that's a funny thing to say to someone that you've just met.

It turned out that her daughter, Angelica, was at the same school as Jack in Meopham. They knew one another. And then she kept leaving Angelica at weekends because she was having therapy or something. (She was probably in rehab, if you ask me). And now she's buggered off to India to see a guru called Bodo or something who's going to "realign her chakras". What a lot of piffle. She's left me an email address and I feel like sending her a message telling her what a lot of codswallop it all is.

Jack and Angelica spent the whole of this evening gazing silently in to their hand-held devices, their little fingers massaging the screens as if they were holding delicate animals in their hands. I wish they would read books. I asked them to tidy their rooms but it was as if they had been struck deaf and dumb and I harrumphed back to my study and poured myself a chilled glass of *muy seco*. I think I write better in the evenings. Roll on winter. One can conjure the medieval world more easily by firelight.

Looking round my study walls, I have always found old Ninian's painting of *Mount Ararat from Yerevan* quite disturbing. Of course it was a gift from Belinda.

Another text message from Belinda: *Changing planes in Chicago. Love you.* I thought: great, I'll catch you while you've got a signal. So I pressed the little Belinda icon on my iPhone and immediately got through to her voice mail. I heard Belinda say: *Sorry I can't take your call right now...*

I said: *It's me, darling. Nothing really – just checking if you got my previous voicemail about Jack's football match? Don't work too hard. Love you.*

Another ping. Oh, it' a text message from Jack who is all of twenty metres away from where I'm sitting now at my desk right now. He asks: *What's for supper?* Christ, I thought they said they had already eaten at a friend's house.

I told them: *Here's a fiver each - now piss of down to MacDonald's.* It's far too far to walk there, they said. (Come to think of it, the nearest one is about nine miles away). You'll have to take us in your car. I can't, I said, I've had a few drinks. Angelica looked at me with exactly the same expression that Varina wore that time she told me I'd committed a terrible crime in a previous life. Only more so.

***

There has been a drowning. A body has been found floating in the river Medway. It appears a man fell from Aylesford Bridge. But how is the mysterious stranger implicated? Father Leofranc is suspicious.

I hope nobody thinks it's too *Name of the Rose*.

***

I walk down the corridor which leads from my study to the garden room – the one that Belinda rather grandly calls our *Hall of Fame*. There are photos of us all at various moments in our lives. There is Belinda, in easy joviality with Hilary Clinton; and there is Xan meeting the Dalai Lama. This one is Old Ninian with the Prince of Wales who – I'm not supposed to let this be known – purchased a number of Ninian's larger canvasses which are now displayed at Birkhall. Here is Jack lifting his football trophy last year; and this one is of me making a keynote address to the *Society of Kent Librarians'* Christmas Dinner. Come to think of it, I do look a bit pissed in that one.

Belinda's mother was American *Old Money*, of course. Her uncle was a Senator. She is much more at home in America than I am. There are no standing stones there. Her father was the English landscape painter, the late Sir Ninian Crane. To be absolutely honest, I've never really liked Ninian's paintings. Too brooding.

Christ! I don't believe it. An email from Varina...

Sorry, darlings but Bodo says it's going to take more like three months than three weeks to sort out my chakras – I'm sure Angelica won't mind. She adores staying with Jack.

I have a good mind to write back by return something rude. But one thing life has taught me – never to reply to emails after half a bottle of sherry.

I'm going to tell Belinda exactly what I think, though. I mean the cheek of it. I'm writing her an email now expressing my total dismay at Varina's presumption. I know that Belinda will look at it from my perspective.

Two hours later: ping. *In LA - Hyatt Regency. That's great - Jack will be thrilled. xxx*

I didn't know Belinda was going to California. I might give Olivia, Belinda's PA, a call in the morning just to find out her schedule. On the other hand, Olivia got very cagey with me last time I did that. And Belinda scolded me later for trying "to mother" her.

When I picked up Jack and Angelica from school the first thing they said to me in stereo was: *What's for dinner tonight*? I've got out all the old Keith Floyd books and I'm enjoying a quick slurp while I marinate some chicken. I'm even wearing the chef's apron Belinda bought for me in Harrods. The creatures are gazing into their devices once more and probably haven't even noticed.

Angelica told me over dinner – which was a triumph, by the way – not to forget about her ballet lesson tomorrow night in Maidstone. Bloody cheek – the sheer presumption. I have decided to communicate my annoyance to Varina in no uncertain terms.

What I have decided is to write Varina an old-fashioned letter, only in digital form, of course; and to send it to the ashram with instructions that they should print it off and deliver it to her in paper form. That will have a superior impact.

***

A productive morning. I have composed an elegant and witty letter to Varina in which I insinuate quite pointedly that Angelica's best interests would be served by her mother's immediate return. I have also knocked out a brooding chapter in which a young girl of about Angelica's age (and who, funnily enough, shares her long golden tresses) is flung by the psychopath down the village well by night. They wanted dark, didn't they? I'm going to send my emails later.

I must pop down to Waitrose – we're running low on sherry.

So I drop little Angelica at the ballet school in Maidstone and do you know what she said to me? *Don't drink while you're waiting for me – you've got to drive me home.* Have you ever had two hours to kill in Maidstone on a

Wednesday evening and not been allowed to go to a pub? What the hell is one supposed to do? There is the library, mind you. I wanted to check up on the history of flooding in the Medway Valley in the late fourteenth century. Oh goodie – I feel a moment of killer research is about to precipitate itself.

Sod it. *Library closed on Wednesday evenings*. Thanks, Varina

An email from Belinda. *This deal is going to take longer than expected. There's going to be an announcement in the Financial Times tomorrow. Must dash – I've got an interview with Richard Quest on CNN*. Oh, don't worry, love. I've got better things on my mind. Like the outbreak of bubonic plague which has hit Canterbury. Not to mention cooking the children's dinner.

The Archbishop has fled to his palace in Maidstone.

I came across a disturbing report on a news website this evening. Xan has gone missing in the mountains of Eastern Turkey. I knew he was planning to write a book about *The Flood*. I am sure he will turn up. A few years back everyone presumed him dead when he went missing in the Kalahari Desert. Four months later, a group of trekkers found him living with the Hottentot. He had already learnt their click-based language and was an ace hunter. He then made an amazing film for TV about his Hottentot blood brother.

They ate my lasagne verde in silence and then returned noiselessly to their small screens. Time to catch up with my emails over a glass of claret.

Shit! I don't believe it! I've attached the wrong document to the email I sent to the ashram earlier, FAO Varina. How can I have been so stupid? I've attached, *not* my letter to Varina, but the chapter about the little girl being tossed down the well - with instructions to print it out.

She is going to think I'm totally weird. Or worse, she might think that I'm a secret psychopath and tell the police. In the blink of an eye, my home will be pullulating with burly officers dismantling my hard drives. What to do? Think, man, think.

***

The body floating in the Medway and washed ashore near the village of Wouldham was wearing the distinctive doublet and hosiery of a nobleman of the Court of Charles The Wise. A secretary to the Bishop of Rochester declares that he was carrying a heavy purse of golden ducats and some confidential letters which shall be impounded by the church in favour of His Majesty. The plot thickens.

Father Leofranc has had a late-night visitor from Picardy.

***

Dear Sirs, I write pursuant to having submitted an email for the attention of Ms Varina Clarke, who is a British woman resident at your "ashram". Late last night I sent the email for her attention – with some instructions as to how to deliver it - to which was attached a "Word document" which was NOT intended for her perusal. Would you be so kind as to delete the message forthwith –and NOT to print out the attachment as requested?

Most respected Mr Leonard – I, Subash Karma, secretary to His Holiness, "the Bodo", most graciously acknowledge receipt of two emails sent for the attention of honoured Miss Varina. Most sincerely at your service...

Dear Mr Subash - could you confirm that you deleted the said email, as requested, and that Ms Varina did NOT receive a printout of the attachment, as originally requested by an earlier mistake...?

Dear Mr most honourable Leonard – May I first say how gratifying it is to correspond with the author of that most accomplished "oeuvre" (as our French friends would say) "The Pope Must Die". In the state of Uttar Pradesh there are very few members of the intellectual elite who do not possess a copy of this enthralling thriller. (On the other hand, the intellectual elite in this great state of India is somewhat diminutive). I must confess, kind Sir, that, in a previous career, I was a senior "wheel" at the great publishing house of Chakravarty & Subash in Delhi. I hope that you will not hold it against me, dear Mr Leonard, if I inform you that it was I who rejected the said "novel" on the grounds of its inappropriateness for the modern Indian public, who face modern religious-inspired violence on a daily basis...Very sincerely yours...

Dear Mr Subash – I do not hold it against you at all that you rejected a novel that was described by the Daily Mail as "IRA-style choir boys meet The Sopranos in drag". Not a problem. I just need to know – did you delete the email to Miss Varina...?

Kind Mr Leonard – As a matter of professional interest, I took the liberty of printing out the latest chapter of your nascent "oeuvre". HH the Bodo encourages his disciples to seek enlightenment by perfecting the skills they may already have developed in whatever field of experience. I do note a certain change in mood and style in your work which I suspect is motivated by commercialism...Your perception of the English Middle Age was, in your first five novels, somewhat wooden - but authentic...This is crass. Yes, I printed out the chapter in question and burnt it at a special "puja" we had to expurgate demons...Ms Varina is well and is grateful for your kind message of support for her chakra enhancement...PS I have been obliged to tell HH the Bodo about you...

Fuck!

***

This morning I had to get Jack to his football match and Angelica to her riding lesson in two quite separate locations with a twenty minute "time window" between each engagement. I spent over an hour on the internet last night trying *to optimise* my route – largely country lanes, of course. But when I announced to the two demanding clients that I had found a solution, they both regarded me sulkily. Jack said he wanted to get to the football ground earlier to practise with his mates, and Angelica said she didn't want to hang around in the cold.

Sometime between late Mrs Thatcher and early Mr Cameron, "parenting" became a subtle skill-set requiring huge application to achieve. My parents' generation, and all of their forebears, just got on with the autochthonous task of dragging up their progeny. Now, parenting requires advanced negotiation skills, extreme emotional intelligence, financial planning (usually involving spreadsheets), and a PhD in logistics. No wonder most parents feel like total failures.

To be honest, that is probably why I feel so at home in the middle ages. It must have felt so free to have no choice. Mind you, I am really drawn to the *later* middle ages, when communications exploded. Before about 1100 most people, even aristos, lived out their lives without ever receiving a message. And then people started writing to one another again, just as they did in the ancient world. The chatter began: and it has been getting louder ever since.

***

The plague has reached Dartford. It is reported that the royal cortege, heading down Watling Street towards Canterbury has diverted to a hell-hole called Swanley in order to avoid the pestilent town. They find the latrines there squalid. The Archbishop has closed the gates of Maidstone. A Cardinal Rossinelli, the "Pope's Messenger", as some call him, has landed in Dover. Something is up!

***

I stumbled (actually that is probably a dishonest verb) across Jack's **Facebook** page. He styles himself, amongst many claims about his football triumphs, as being *in a relationship with Angelica Clarke*. I find Angelica's page, and – how predictable – she's *in a relationship* with Jack.

I don't quite know how to feel about this. I mean, it is actually rather sweet: young love, and all that. But, for God's sake – they're just kids. I hope they are not doing anything inappropriate together. (They insisted on staying in the oasthouse, which Belinda restored as our "guest wing"). Should I say something? Should I go in there and do what my mother would have done to me? Not that I had a girlfriend at fourteen. In fact, I didn't have a girlfriend until I met Belinda. I was so academic.

Maybe I'll ask Anca tomorrow if she has any ideas what's going on. Maybe not – Romanians are so conservative.

Belinda would probably know what to do. But, right now, I don't think I shall bother her with this.

There's a rather dry rosé in the (secret) wine chiller. Cheers, Belinda! May you get your deal!

This afternoon I found myself in the *John Lewis Food Hall* in Bluewater, where there are some very appealing promotions in the "wine cellar". (It is not at all cellar-like). Having selected a number of quite interesting numbers – with the help of a talkative man with an Oxford accent whose baldness was disguised by a woolly hat – I proceeded to the checkout. I could not help but notice the newspapers on display, though I normally tend to avoid them as they distract me from the late fourteenth century. The *Financial Times* proclaimed:

MEGADEAL AIMS TO REVOLUTIONISE GLOBAL COMMUNICATIONS

There was a problem with a malfunctioning debit card two customers ahead of me. So I began to read.

The communications billionaire Larry Wiseman has announced a mega-merger which will secure control for his conglomerate, WiseReach, of the global internet, artificial intelligence hubs and robot production industries...International lawyer, Belinda Crane said: This is a historic deal which will leave the world a smaller, but a wealthier place...

***

The royal cortege has reached Maidstone. Archbishop Odo has ordered that the gates be opened. Cardinal Rosinelli is sheltering at the Archbishop's lodgings in Wye. The scribes are frantic, with messages in code being sent by horsemen across the Wield...

***

Well, that's bloody weird. Anca has a left a note on my desk saying that she's resigned. How the hell am I supposed to keep this place clean? That is so bloody selfish of her.

I call Olivia. I have not heard from my wife for over a week. It's not Olivia, it's a stand-in called Vanessa. I am correct but firm with her – where is my wife? She says: *Well, she's with Larry, of course – don't you watch the news?*

***

That Archbishop Odo is a total shit. He has just hurled a platter of lampreys at a page - young Jacopo (a sweet young man who reminds me of Pavel) because Jacopo didn't bow low enough. He's an obesely fat bastard with a carbuncular nose. He might be scheming and good at arse-licking in royal circles but my God, the man is vile. A very fine scholar, mind you. He can even read Aramaic.

He has left poor Jacopo bleeding and in tears before flouncing out of the dining chamber.

***

I don't believe this. I'm just coming to the much anticipated meeting between Archbishop Odo and Cardinal Rossinelli in Maidstone Palace. It's a critical scene in which the purpose of the Cardinal's visit is revealed. And the subtleties of personality – twisted and gifted – of these princes of the Church come into play. And guess what?

Pavel has appeared outside my study windows with a ridiculous blowing machine slung over his shoulder which he is using to arrange the fallen leaves into amenable piles. CHRIST, the noise!

I am trying to gesticulate to Pavel through the leaded panes that he should go away, but he can't see me as his back is turned as he removes offending leaves from Belinda's precious herbaceous borders around the lawn of the rose garden. I open one of the window panes and begin shouting to him but then I realise that he is wearing ear-protecting muffs (or whatever they call them in *B&Q*). Come to think of it, I did instruct Pavel to buy one of these machines last week on my credit card. But I had no idea these ludicrous devices could be so ear-splittingly bloody loud.

This is driving me insane – I had mentally constructed a very subtle (and barbed) little speech of welcome by Archbishop Odo, but now I cannot even think above the din. How can I get the wretched young man's attention?

In desperation, I pick up a book lying on my desk – Pevsner's *The Architecture of Kent,* no less – and hurl it manfully in Pavel's direction. I was never good at cricket at school and detested fielding. My schoolmates never let up on their jibes about my eye for a ball. And yet that copy of Pevsner arcs through the air and – God dammit – it lands squarely on Pavel's muffed head. And he collapses to the ground like a rag doll...

Oh my God, the penny has dropped. This happens to writers sometimes. You write things and then realise in a *Eureka moment* their meaning later. That Archbishop Odo lost control because he loves Jacopo, but knows that the young man finds him repulsive.

In fact, Archbishop Odo is turning out to be one of my more fascinating character-creations. A low orphan, he is marked out from an early age by his cunning and sheer animal intelligence. He is allowed by the Abbott of Dartford Priory to work in the priory as a kitchen boy. But, in time, the Abbott allows him access to his library...And then, bewitched by the brilliance of his mind and his infectious charm...his bed. Oh dear, I hope I haven't upset Simon's "demographic". Tough. But at last, I'm finding my voice. (*The Pope Must Die* was, I admit, a bit formulaic).

Bodo and Odo? Funny coincidence of names. Whose mind is controlling whom?

Oh my God, a "round robin" email from Varina. She has sent it to about forty people. I wonder who *sillypriscl2 is*. Come to think of it, who is *sillypriscl1*? Or does one really want to know?

Hi Guys! I guess you've been wondering how I've been getting on in India. I know some of you loves were worried. Well, I'm fine. In fact I'm great. You know, this is just about the best experience I've ever had in my life. In fact – drumroll, please – I think, at last, I've found myself. You see, The Bodo (my wonderful guru) has made The Path straightforward. He explained early on that self-realisation is not about perfection. It's largely about understanding your own imperfection. You have to embrace all your past mistakes and failures and regrets and just accept that as part of the bundle of experiences that makes you who you are. When you let go of self-criticism and regrets about your past, you lose any foreboding for the future. That's the pre-condition of flow – living as the Creator intended we should live – being ourselves. It's so damn liberating – I just can't tell you how much better and happier I feel. Mind you, some of my chakras are still blocked – but, don't worry – the Bodo says he has a technique for me that never fails...

And so it continued until I had a sudden urge to press the *Delete* button. I mean, is anyone supposed to find this interesting? And no bloody mention of her daughter, Angelica, whom I have protected and preserved for nearly two months now without so much as a Thank You! That woman is mad.

I wonder who Angelica's father was. From what gossip I get in *The George*, Angelica's was most certainly not a virgin birth. Apparently, Varina told Belinda during one of their late-night lady-sessions that Angelica was conceived at a Zen Buddhist monastery on the slopes of Mount Fuji. Varina was attending a meditation retreat which was also attended by a beautiful blonde young man. That night he came to her cell. But, since they were subject to a solemn vow of silence for the duration of the retreat, the two lovers never even disclosed to one another any information at all, not even their names. The next morning the beautiful young man had mysteriously left.

Only Varina could come up with a story like that.

I don't bloody believe it! Modern children are ghastly. Angelica and Jack (probably in that order) have sent me to Coventry! They are refusing to speak to me at all and are only communicating by text message, if you please. And my crimes? This is monstrous. Angelica advises me in a poorly punctuated message that I drink too much and that I have a very nasty temper! And I have been so kind to that motherless waif. I mean, excuse me? I'm just the bloke who, while trying to write a highly experimental novel set in the middle ages, ferries them backwards and forwards in a nice motor and then cooks them gourmet meals which they then leave. (I always donate the leavings to Anca and Pavel; I am such a bloody kind boss).

What does one do? I mean, one can't slap youngsters these days as my parents would have done, more's the pity. And I hate the way that they are on their moral high horses all the time. What do they know of life? Well, no more lifts and gourmet meals until they show a little more respect...

Apparently, a *Bodo* is (and I quote) *a supreme being who has achieved perfect self-realisation who chooses to return from Paradise in order to show the unrealised The Way.* So why does he need a pink Rolls Royce?

Anca has re-appeared and resumed her duties as if her note was never sent. She has been crying. Bloody Hell! That gives me an idea...Jacopo, you're back in the novel, mate.

I forgot to mention that I was terribly contrite about what happened to Pavel, who is such a sweet-natured and good looking young man. In fact, I rushed out, abandoning my work station during writing time (as jobbing writers should never do) to resuscitate him. Well, I must say that he didn't look that injured to me, despite all the histrionic groaning in Polish – or was it Lithuanian?

Pavel has since told me about his origins. He was born in a part of Russia that used to be part of Germany. During Soviet times, they moved to Lithuania. But his cousins lived in Poland (Mazurian Lakes – which sound romantic, if icy in winter). And after independence – and his father's early death - he moved there with his mother and grandmother. Then, hey presto, all borders fell and they translated themselves to England. Now he is worried about "Brexit". (I am sure that Archbishop Odo would have done well on this topic on *Question Time*). It must be so confusing to be an Eastern European.

I am beginning to regret having asked Pavel to lie down on my bed until he recovered. I received a delegation this evening from Angelica and Jack who told me they were *quite cool about my relationship with Pavel, given the way that Belinda had treated me.*

Bloody Hell! They always seem to know more than I do.

It's nice that they are talking to me again, though. And no, I told them, I am many things, but I've not thought of myself as gay for years – at least since that summer when I lived with Xan in Paris. I recall that Belinda turned up and prosecuted a breathless affair with Xan who suddenly dropped both of us for that Japanese martial artist fellow. Those two fled to Tokyo. Belinda, still madly in love with Xan (as I was), proposed to me. We married at once and about one year later, Jack arrived.

As a young man, Xan often talked of death. Once, at the climax of our intimacy, he told me that if ever he went before me, he would send an angel to watch over me.

A message to Belinda.

Belinda – I'd really like to know what's up. I think you owe me a window in your schedule to speak properly. I'm on Skype now.

Within seconds the Skype function on my laptop splutters into life with lots of weird, underwater bells. I place my large glass of Mersault behind the machine so that it may not be held against me.

Belinda's face appears on the screen. There are pallid mountains behind her, massaged by fragile early morning sunshine. She looks tired. She begins to speak: *Leonard, I'm so sorry...*

Where are you?

Hawaii...

But at precisely that point her image freezes into a passable impression of Munch's *The Scream*. There is no sound. A message appears on the bottom left corner of my screen. *Interrupted signal.*

And yet I feel that I have heard all I want to hear. I knew this Larry person would be a bad influence.

So I flick the key of the remote control and conjure up *Newsnight.*

It's Evan Davies smilingly trying to engage a kind of wolf-man with a thick black mane and an expression of infinite superiority.

He says: *Look, Evan. You've missed the point. It's about the future potential of human communication. We're already there on the technology side. We have implanted chips into chimps' brains which tell them when to eat and when to sleep. The human brain is an analogue to a chimp's brain.*

It's how we decide to use this technology that matters. So don't blame me: blame progress...

I switch off the TV in disgust and notice that my iPhone is flashing. Of course, it's a message from Belinda.

It reads: *I'm so very sorry, Leonard. I'm with Larry now. We both knew that something like this would happen. We have both moved on. Don't worry: you can have the rectory and the million or so in our joint account. I'd never want to hurt you. We can talk about Jack's future later. B*

***

My God. This Cardinal Rossinelli is a bastard too! He only comes to England demanding that the appointment of English bishops be repatriated to Rome. Apparently, so the increasingly wary Archbishop Odo learns, the Pope believes that some English bishops are engaged in witchcraft. How typically European! But of course he has another agenda – as our brilliant English Odo surmises. Who will outfox whom? I think I know...

How fortunate that the King contracted the palsy in Swanley and had to retreat to Winchester. He would only have made things worse. Now, my Odo is in total charge of England's future.

***

Of course, I want to apologise profusely to the terrible twins when they finally come back from school in the back of some gleaming black four-by-four driven by a local mother who just offers a kind of royal wave from behind tinted glass. They are oddly conciliatory.

Am I feeling OK? Was I alright this morning? And my question: how the bugger did they even get to school without me?

Yes, I admit it: I got wasted last night. But it really wasn't my fault. After I got that message from Belinda I repaired to the master bedroom, forgetting that I had left the wounded Pavel to sleep it off in the four-poster. And there he was, sitting up in bed, smiling shirtless with a bottle of vodka.

Personally, I am a wine man: I have never really liked vodka. But then when drunk ice-cold in tiny glasses it becomes quite festive. The signifier of a special moment in Eastern European life. Actually, Pavel must have had more than one bottle. He might even have found the bin in my secret dressing room.

I am determined not to apologise to these fourteen year old "children" (if that is indeed what they are – in mediaeval times there was no such concept of childhood). But Jack puts his arms around me – for the first time in years – and he says: *We understand.* I begin to blub. Emotional intelligence maybe; pity about the common sense.

***

Actually, the King turns out not to be a total plonker, as readers may have supposed. He had intercepted all those secret messages sent across the Wield. And he has a certain young spy (code name "J") there in the secret meeting between Archbishop Odo and Cardinal Rossinelli. Oh dear, I fear that Odo's bright star may be about to fall...
***

I simply don't think I can take this anymore. A message from Varina. But clearly not intended for me. Rather, she has evidently mistaken my email address for Belinda's –

and they are, admittedly, very similar. But I simply wish this had not happened. I want to crawl into a hole.

Darling Belinda – good on you for you for your great news! Atta girl! And do you know where I am on the love curve? I mean, I've just got to tell somebody. I'm having a frenetic love-bash with my guru, Bodo. The sex is just amazing. It's off-the-clock. I mean I didn't even realise that I was multi-orgasmic before. So much for my English lovers...This super-man is not just a healer but a stallion...

If I am ever arraigned in court for the crime of a lack of aesthetic aptitude I shall indeed admit that I did read further of this inconsequential smut. Let us just say that Varina's stock plunged even further on the bourse of human estimation. And I felt stunned that a woman of Belinda's stature – my Belinda – could be fodder for this tripe. Whatever the children do know, I hope that they are spared the foul-smelling entrails of Varina' inanity.

By the way, those two have been very nice of late – though I am still concerned about what they might make of Pavel's new status. Angelica actually cooked me dinner this evening – with a little help from Jack. Spag Bol. But, actually, rather tasty. Angelica, who clutches the key of the wine chiller like a medieval gaoler (bless her), served me a small glass of rosé. Little does she know that I have a rather nice bin in my dressing room (where children never go).

In an idle moment I couldn't help typing "the Bodo" into *Google Images*. A photo of a large fat hairless face came up. He looks like a superannuated accountant from

Mumbai (which is apparently exactly what he is). No, he looks like a tortoise that's had Botox.

Something that Jack let slip today leads me to suppose that those two are not as innocent as I might have assumed. He referred to mothers disappointing their children. Was he referring to his mother or Angelica's? Or both, perhaps? The problem is that I don't know what they know.

Come to think of it: they probably do know more than I know.

No, I don't feel particularly despondent about Belinda. Hurt, yes. I think fondly of our days punting on the Cam and those summer afternoons on the Left Bank and thank whatever force of nature gave us those moments in the first place. Plus Jack, who was – sincerely – an unexpected blessing. To be honest, I am more worried about Archbishop Odo, who has now gravely incurred the King's displeasure. Saintly Father Leofranc, it now seems, was an agent provocateur. Cardinal Rossinelli's mission to England was a giant sting.

I'm gripped. I hope my readers will be too. Plotting is futile - character is destiny.

Blimey, the woman driving the black four-by-four with the royal wave now takes Jack and Angelica to school and does all the ballet and football logistics. That's amazingly helpful, given the pressure I'm under at the moment. I chased the black polished charabanc down the drive this morning and tapped on the driver's tinted window as the car slowed at the gate. The window purred down by three inches. *Yes, Mr Norman*, a lady-voice said, *We know everything…*

***

Documents provided by the Bishop of Rochester (who has always hated Odo) have precipitated the Archbishop's fall. He has been arraigned by the Star Chamber for treason. During an interview he is prodded by the Earl of Wessex. He attests to the many services that he has rendered the Church, England and the Crown. The nobles jeer…

***

I knew this was going to happen. A message from Belinda:

Larry wants to meet Jack. He's sending a private jet. Please let Jack have his passport.

I don't know why Pavel – who has now fully recovered from his (very minor) injury – feels entitled to use my private bathroom all the time. Even Belinda wouldn't do that – but then she has another, even bigger, bathroom down the corridor. I mean, bathrooms are sacred spaces – aren't they? Mind you, I wouldn't have wanted to have shared Archbishop Odo's bathroom. And in the Tower of London, the poor man is reduced to a bucket.

Angelica and Jack have texted, asking "to meet me for a conversation". This is worse than the middle ages.

There was a slightly snotty review of *Altars of Blood* in *The Spectator* this week. I had almost forgotten it was released last month. *Mr Norman traipses through the middens of late medieval England in a pair of Hush Puppies…* To think that supposedly intelligent people are paid to write this rubbish.

I was trying to write the scene where the King unexpectedly visits Odo for in the Tower during his trial for treason. It's critical because they are both bound to one another in enduring ways but their relationship is unravelling due to forces beyond either's control. But I just can't get that hideous mistakenly received email from Varina out of my mind. The thought of her in sexual congress with a cosmetically-enhanced tortoise is just too distracting.

Those two sleek conspirators glide into my study. I am at my desk, like some mock-Victorian paterfamilias. Before they deliver words that I suspect have been carefully rehearsed, I raise the palm of my right hand and open the small drawer of my desk with the left.

Before you go any further – I have your passport here, Jack. There it is. Please use it as you think fit. There is a world out there. You are a man now.

Actually, he is only fourteen and it was just a year ago that I was fretting about Jack's four days at *Parents Get Lost*!

I must have wrong-footed them. They were obviously expecting a struggle. It is Angelica, as ever, who, after a moment of intense reflection, begins to speak.

That's exactly what we wanted to talk to you about, Leo. Jack doesn't want to go to America to meet that horrid man. And neither do I. Belinda said I should come too. But we don't want to. We want to stay here with you. We want to spend Christmas with you – as a family.

Well, blimey, I wasn't expecting that. You see, at the end of the day, good parenting (actually good fathering) has its own rewards. I feel a glass of something bubbly is in order. Cheers!

Funny, but Xan used to call me Leo.

I have kept meaning to ask Anca why she almost always looks as if she has just been sobbing – it's an awful look…But, hang on, a message from Simon. This is important.

We've tried out the first six chapters on our focus group – and they LOVE it. They are gagging to read more. I think you may have a winner here. Could we have the final MS before Christmas? Cheers, Si…

I suppose reading history at Cambridge was what made me what I am. Early on I just fell in fascinated love with the Crusades. That second long summer vac I managed to get as far as Krac des Chevaliers in Syria with dear old Xan. We got terribly drunk on arak and caused a bit of a stir in a local guest house. To think that all those people have now been bombed to smithereens. It's heart-breaking. But what is the point in eating one's heart out about the here-and now? What really matters is the past. I suspect that Pavel feels like that too. He said something the other day about his people jumping frontiers over centuries like skipping ropes.

It's the second Sunday of Advent and – here's a first – Jack and Angelica joined me for candlelit evensong at that gorgeous, delicate Norman church at Luddesdown. It nestles in a still wooded gentle fold in the Downs. The village it once served was emptied by the Black Death. (You couldn't make it up). What did Eliot say about *the dusky church at smoke fall*?

Christmas is upon us and they have taken it upon themselves to organise the festivities. Great. Apparently, I shall be in charge of Christmas dinner – which will *not* be turkey, an American bird that was not eaten in England before the late nineteenth century. I might go for fish cooked with herbs from a mediaeval kitchen garden. Pavel favours carp – another non-indigenous species. I think I have a project coming on: *The Dartford Priory Cook Book*. Or maybe not.

I finally caught up with Anca and confronted her. Well, actually, while she was dusting the library, I asked her if she would join me for a chilled flute of Champagne. (*Pol Roger* – Churchill's favourite). (Angelica absent-mindedly left the wine chiller key in the lock this morning). She didn't need much persuading. Then I popped the question: What was troubling her?

She must have got through my entire stock of tissues this afternoon. Basically – as a novelist I do find this plot a bit predictable – her fiancé and childhood sweetheart, to whom she has been betrothed since she was about twelve, has run off with the beauty queen from the village just up the road in northern Transylvania.

What does one say to someone with a broken heart? *Care for another glass of bubbly*?

No, I am not heartless, really. I spent most of the afternoon trying to comfort her. We had a little walk over the fields, down past the windmill, over the megalithic burial mound to the vineyard, talking about this and that – though she was continuously lapsing into Romanian – or was it Hungarian, as she speaks both?

Sorry, Si, but the deadline looks challenging. What did the great Douglas Adams say about deadlines? Oh yes: *I love the whooshing sound they make as they flash by...*

My regular readers (all twenty of them – there is a **Facebook** page) have grown to expect last-minute twists. Of course dear old fatty Odo was not a traitor – he was stitched up. And an unlikely ally has emerged who has, it seems, the ear of an insider at court...

Angelica has invited Anca to move into the oasthouse and is "managing" her. Anca has seemed much happier this last week. Say what you like about young Angelica, she is quite business-like. I suppose that growing up without a father and a fruitcake mother like Varina she has just been forced to get on with things – a bit like Pavel's forebears (though I don't think they would have put up with Varina). She has even managed to get Jack to take a more serious attitude towards his homework – something that even Belinda could not achieve with her carrot-and-stick offensive. I had always assumed that Jack had more respect for Belinda than he had for me. I am not so sure now. I suspect that he found both of us dysfunctional – and then Angelica appeared.

Blimey, Anca actually cooked dinner tonight, involving dumplings. I am sure she knows where the key to my wine chiller is kept. She seems happier. As I passed through the kitchen for a top-up just now I couldn't help but notice that she was humming some kind of exotic lullaby.

The lady driving the polished black four-by-four is the mother of one of Jack's football chums. They are local landowners with a silly double-barrelled name – something like Blenkinsop-Cholmondeley. At least old money is generally non-judgmental. Not like the tykes in the George who started sniggering in corners when I popped in for a pint the other day.

I was expecting Belinda to send me a message along the lines of *You've poisoned Jack's mind against me*. But no such message came. In fact, there is no news from America at all. Come to think of it, I am actually quite worried about Belinda.

I ring Belinda's PA: Olivia or Vanessa, it matters not. May I know where my "wife" may be contacted? There is a lot of stone-walling and telephone silences, and eventually the line goes dead. And they are supposed to be one of the world's top law firms. Most odd.

Today was my forty-first birthday and I received a sweet card from the young people, though nothing from Belinda.

This evening I have re-read Xan's book about his walk through Tibet with his spiritual guide, Nodo. It is a masterpiece. There is an unforgettable scene where they are lost on a mountain pass in poor weather - and at that moment they are set upon by a pack of ravening wolves. Nodo chants some ancient Tibetan incantation and the wolves become calm. Then the wolves walk ahead of them, turning their heads around as if to beckon them forward. The beasts lead them to a cave where they take shelter from the snowstorm. Whatever I write, I will never achieve anything to compare with this.

***

That wonderful young man, Jacopo, eventually manages to petition the King on Odo's behalf. He knows the Archbishop to be a noble prince of the Church whose name has been grievously besmirched by malicious foreign powers...

***

My word: an email from the clam-like Olivia.

I am so sorry to be the person to inform you about this, Mr Norman – you are obviously not reading the newspapers - but when the recent so-called mega-deal ran into difficulties your wife Ms Crane was accused of malpractice and has now left the employment of Morton Chambers. I am sending this message via my personal email and would be grateful if you do not reply as we are not supposed to discuss firm activities on personal media. I know that you are a writer and that you have your mind on other stuff. By the way, my boyfriend Darren loved "Altars of Blood" but he says he worked out that the murderer was the bishop in chapter one. Love, Olivia xx

Mrs Cholmondeley-Blenkinsop, or whatever her name is, actually lowered the electric window and waved to me this morning as she accelerated down the drive in the jet black machine. I was trying to install new set of duck houses by the pond with Pavel who seems to have moved in. He says there is no accommodation in the village, anyway. And one of the plebs at the George was obnoxious to him.

I'm even more worried about Belinda. But then I think Varina's silence is also strange.

And then a second mistaken message from Varina, intended for Belinda. But this one is entirely different in tone from the ghastly bonking message. I scroll down and I realise that this message is a reply to a message that Belinda sent Varina yesterday. Oh my God, I knew this. But I skim.

He's a total monster. His rages are apocalyptic. No one can disagree with him. He starts by undermining your confidence in subtle, almost imperceptible ways. And then he is hurling priceless ceramics at you...And I have lost my job because of him – and my family...

I know, darling. I've had a similar experience here. The Bodo persuaded me that I could only unloop my chakras through Tantric sex. And then, half way through my "therapy" he began "to cure" a contemptible American blonde midget...He hasn't even spoken to me for weeks...I have been consigned to menial kitchen chores as part of my so-called "self-subjugation" practice...

I suppose Odo would be exasperated by the pickles that women get themselves into. But then Saint Angela (who appears in *Altars of Blood*) would say that it is the men that entice poor women into such pickles. Of course, I have absolutely no opinion on the matter whatsoever.

It is the fourth Sunday of Advent and I have almost finished the novel.

***

The scene where Jacopo, now a companion of the King, goes to the Tower to tell the fetid Odo that he will be freed forthwith is such a tender epiphany that tears actually rolled down my cheeks as I tapped the keyboard. Their roles have been reversed; and Odo owes his life to Jacopo's diplomacy.

Anca bought in a large sherry on a silver tray (Angelica permits Anca to serve me drinkies after six) and saw the tears. *Mr Leonard, you okay*? she asked. *Very fine, my dear Anca – but you have forgotten the olives.*

Oh yes, and Cardinal Rossinelli has been chucked down a well – apparently a random attack by a medieval psychopath. What bad luck. Or is it? Anyway, one must tie up loose ends.

***

I am in my study having now re-reviewed the manuscript. There is disco   -beat music – *Time of My Life* – pullulating in bursts from the garden room, interspersed with loud peals of youthful laughter. I have encouraged Pavel to do most what he loves. So we converted the garden room into a makeshift dance studio. This morning he has been taking Jack and Angelica through some classic dance routines. They love it. And they adore him. But then he is rather wonderful. I had forgotten how sweet life can be – just like that long hot summer of 2001.

But may it last, this time.

I submitted the manuscript on the Monday morning and have endured nearly two days of internet silence. Angelica and Jack are working on the Christmas tree. Mrs Cholmondeley-Four-by-Four has invited us all for drinks after church on Christmas morning. Angelica seems to have her eating out of her palm. I have to admit that little Angelica is a good networker – much better than I am. Or Jack is.

Oh, no! I've just caught a headline on the web. *Explorer Xan Channing dies on the slopes of Mount Ararat*. It seems that he was climbing in winter alone but for the company of his long-time Turkish "guide". I feel a stab of pain but reflect that Xan's life was the unbelievable adventure that he dreamed of at Cambridge – a dream which came true. Belinda, like me, will take this news badly.

Xan's life was a message to humanity the true meaning of which shall only be deciphered in time.

Christmas Eve. Jack, Angelica and I (and Pavel and Anca, would you believe?) are going to a carol service later. We shall open our presents before Christmas lunch tomorrow. (I suspect that this may actually be served after the Queen's Speech, given the size of the suckling pig, which only just fits into the Aga). But tonight we shall open our cards. (I am sure that my mother would not have approved, but these young people are adamant).

The children (but should I still call them that? - for they seem so very mature) offer me a card that I open with both hands (having nestled my wine glass in the inglenook).

Dear Dad – we love you and are very proud of you.

I am embracing them when my iPhone goes berserk. A moment of blissful intimacy is shattered by a light flashing and electronic chimes. It's Simon from Heinrich and Steadman.

Just want to let you know that we're in a bidding war for this one and we're already well above seven figures. They are talking film rights. Good news: you're in the money. Bad news: clear your diary. We need you for every book fair and literary love-fest ASAP. Car coming to get you 08:00, 03 January. Merry Christmas, Si. PS: Can you get us the outline of the sequel by, say, mid-Jan?

It's nothing, I say to the children.

And then Anca presses her card into my hand.

To the most wonderful English gentleman, Mr Leonard, who has saved a poor Romanian girl's life...

Bloody Hell! That hand-held device is going bonkers again. This time it's — I don't believe it — Mr Subash from the "ashram".

Most honoured Mr Leonard; it is I, Mr Subash, formerly of Chakravarty & Subash, a most distinguished Delhi-based publisher, and now Personal Secretary to HH The Bodo. I wish to inform you, kind Sir, that the reason why the Miss Varina has not responded to your messages is that she fled from this holy place some five days ago. I must tell you that the said Miss Varina left, as you might say, "under a cloud". It seems that she now — if you will forgive me a somewhat indelicate expression now used, I believe in contemporary English — is "batting for the other side". She made a series of most inappropriate advances towards female members of our kitchen staff. And then she took a blunt instrument to the sacred onyx lingam in our shrine room. We are advised that Ms Varina boarded an India Airlines flight from New Delhi to New York yesterday...

I ask those two who regard me quizzically. *Did you know that Varina is en route for America?*

Were those smirks?

More flashing lights and dulcet counter-tenor tones (my new ringtone is a Florentine madrigal): Belinda.

Don't worry about me. I'm in New York looking for work. A dear and wise friend has arrived to support me. We've already found, with Uncle's help, a lovely apartment on the Upper East Side. We can't resume the life we had before, Leonard. Jack and Angelica can visit soon if they want to – for now they're keeping their distance...

Then Pavel steps forward and presses his card into my hands.

My darling Leo, you have made me whole again. And I can make you whole. Let's be together...

He crushes me in a *bear-hug*. The children laugh. I feel that any crimes of my past lives have been absolved.

And we all pile into the German machine, Pavel at the wheel, and wend our way down the country lanes to the little church in Luddesdown, through dancing snowflakes. Services only take place here at Christmas now. How lucky I am to have not just a fine son but also a remarkable daughter. In the darkness, I can make out her determined little face regarding me with a look of deep affection, tempered by mild disapproval. By what mysterious rules of chance she came into my life, I shall probably never know. For one so young, she has a rare capacity for silence.

We can worry about the women after Christmas. Belinda always lands on her feet. I'll tell Simon that my assistant will be coming with me to the literary jamborees. And he needs access to a dance studio.

In a flash, I've got the sequel's name. *Clash of Mitres*. That ninny, the Bishop of Rochester, and his pompous friend, the Earl of Wessex, are riding for a fall. My big, fat, clever Odo is back in business. And this time with a cardinal's hat and a bright red frock.

Xan's memorial service is going to be a big affair. Belinda is sure to be there. I can imagine us holding hands in shared grief.

My adopted daughter's piercing blue eyes remind me of someone. In fact, they even seem to smoulder in the darkness – just like…But no, that is an impossibly improbable notion.

Whatever happens, I do need to keep Angelica on-side, though. She's still got the key to my wine chiller.

The Gospel of Vic the Fish

Everything began with words. They are only words, stories. In the end it's what you make of words; at least before we get to Heaven. Sometimes, they're a glimpse of another world. This is just my story, though there are many others. But this one's gospel.

Very glad to meet you. We don't get many visitors these days. My name's Vic Evangelistos, cockney born and bred. Fancy a nice slice of bloater paste on toast?

Summer

Don't talk to me about miracles. The biggest miracle is that we're here at all.

I've lived in East London since my Mum had me back in the War. We were doing fine us two until the flying bomb got us. Thirteenth of June 1944, it was, to be precise. If you don't know what flying bombs were, they were early missiles what the Nazis chucked on London, last ditch-like, to win the War. Well, they didn't win the War in '44, but they did a fine job of our terrace on Grove Road.

My Mum died there and then; but they found me, a nine month old baby, lying in the chimney breast. They reckon my Mum had put me there so I could be safe, since she'd heard it coming. Anyway, it was my Auntie Leenie who took me in and bought me up, like, even though she was what they'd now call *traumatised*. But people in them days, we just got on with it.

You see, my dad had died the year before in that Bethnal Green disaster. I don't think it was the Germans. I think people just trod on one another, as would you do, in a panic, in the dark. *One hundred and fifty three* dead, just like so many fish caught in a net; and no inquest, not for years anyway. But there's a kind of monument there now: a bit weird though, if you ask me.

You might've heard of me. I was that gobby git at Billingsgate fish market, sometimes on the telly, generally known in my heyday, in the roaring the eighties, as *Vic the Fish*. East End fish culture meant so much more than cod and plaice in batter with chips. I mean, it was me what explained to that Keith Floyd on *Floyd in the Fish Market* that monkfish was a marvel of the seas what could be sizzled in wine and garlic as a dish for prince and pauper alike.

He called it Zarzuela fish - but then that's his problem. Or was - he's dead now. I used to booze with him. I like a drink but couldn't keep up with Old Floydy. Had a couple too many, by the end. He was a smashing bloke. I loved him. Rather Keith than bloody Delia, any day.

And don't even get me going on shellfish. I used to be a porter as a boy for the great Tubby Isaacs at his stall in Aldgate East and what he didn't know about whelks you could write on a tramp's napkin – if he had one, if you get me? I used to hang around Aldgate with Tubby's boys – there were about twelve of us, mostly Jewish but some of us, otherwise. I was half Greek, though no one knew. Aunt Leenie once told me that my dad came from an island called Patmos. But all his stuff was destroyed in the fire, so I was never sure.

Tubby's whelk stall *was* the East End. He was a kind of teacher, and he taught me and the other boys everything I know about fish. When I think of Tubby, I smell the salty sweet seaweed scent of seafood, and I know that I'm alive in a world where the good will beat the bad. Just as we cockney nippers beat the Nazis, in the end.

He was always reaching out to people, Tubby. It was Tubby what sponsored me and Reg for the boxing club. That's where we met Ronnie and Reggie. We learned the lot from them. On Saturdays, Tubby would take us boys to *Bloom's*. Oh, the gefilte fish, the soused herring, the pickles teasing my tongue like an high-class tart.

One night in *Bloom's* a woman arrived: it was his Mum. A lovely woman, Maria: she was always kissing and cuddling people – Romanian, she was, or something, always dressed in black lace. This time, she says to Tubby something like: *Why haven't these poor, lovely boys got wine?* When we turned around the water we had been drinking was dark as blood and tasted of bitter-sweet cherries.

We couldn't afford posh restaurants, mate, but we bloody well knew how to eat. When I got my job as a porter, I used to take my Auntie Leenie out, maybe once a month, to *Pellicci* on Bethnal Green Road. She used to order cannelloni and they made it for her especially just like she was some kind of duchess. We used to round it off with *gellati*. I must say, the Italians taught us East Enders a thing or two about how to eat. And the Jews too - and the rest. I'd die these days for masala cod.

I remember once, me and my soul mate Reg were taken by Aunt Leenie on a coach trip to Thanet, led by Tubby. There were all these old folk in the bus as well as young ones like me – this was during the Suez Crisis: they'd launched a war in Egypt. And we broke down outside Whitstable, by the sea wall. Seasalter, it was called. Everyone was hungry, and wandered onto the beach, beholding Sheppey. Yet, somehow, Tubby managed to conjure up a fish meal out of some loaves they'd brought and some wonderful Whitstable pilchards. You don't see many of them no more. No one went hungry. They returned to Stepney changed men, and women - *happy*.

We didn't know what ever happened to Tubby, though I heard it said in Petticoat Lane where they said his brother worked, that Tubby was still alive and living in Thanet. I would have given my all to see him once again.

Well, we may reminisce about the past, but things have changed a fair bit, I might tell you, though on the other hand some big things, like fish, don't change at all. You've got to see things in the round, I always say.

The docks closed, bombed to smithereens by the people who took out my Mum – we bombed them, too, mind, almost to oblivion, but not quite, 'cos they survived to make very fine cars. And as for the docks - they never made money after containers came in. I suppose all our work went to Felixstowe and the like, though I've never met an Essex docker. Towers and buildings rose up where the docks had been – a new kind of money. Eventually even the fish market moved to Canary Wharf. Most of my people went out to Essex, and many even further East. Like Southend, Margate and Australia.

My Aunt Leenie ended up in Melbourne with her man. She died there. I've always wanted to visit her grave, but they tell me it's as hot as hell there. And I couldn't face two days on a bloody aeroplane.

There's still a few of us who stayed. You know what they say: the fool who stays at home, and the fool who goes away. I'm the first type of fool. And may I die so. Except that sometimes people that you love go away, and you must follow.

Who's the fool, then?

When Billingsgate Market moved, they told me: *Evangelistos, you have to lease your space anew*. I applied to this big landlord called the *Poge Trust*. And they told me, basically, sling your hook, mate. They said I had a record. We've all got black marks, if only truth be told. What is the price of a mistake? In my case - everything. If I'd had some kind of posh lawyer, I'd have sued. But what can an humble fishmonger do? I never worked again in, like, a proper job. Though I've always managed to duck and dive.

I worked in the New Billingsgate for a few mates, helping out on their stalls, from time to time, but it was never quite the same. That Mick the Turk was very good to me; he knew I understood fish. But, if you run your own stall, it's yours, and the customers know you. You're like a rabbi; an apostle.

After I retired, if that's the word, I joined the *Action Group* based at St. Paul's Church, on the Roman Road. I was never what you might call a *believer*, but I strongly believe in helping deserving people, which is nearly everyone. I just know that there are little things you can do.

We used to take soup to local old folk, organising day trips to Southend, and that. We even had a boxing club, and though I was past my prime by then, I could still show the lads how to do a great left hook. As could my mate Reg, who'd been a champion in his time.

I still keep Billingsgate hours. In bed by eight and up at half past three. The early morning's always been the best part of the day for me. I take a nap in the afternoon, these days.

Retirement's a funny business. You spend your life running around like a blue-arsed fly and then you've got nothing to do. Just routine: same old, same old.

This is where I live now. *Warden assisted* flats just off the Roman Road, though I don't even feel slightly old. I don't know about the warden though.

Gemma's the name. Silly girl, she's always on the phone and doesn't seem to have any time for us. I don't know who she talks to all the time. But she always waves through the glass and smiles nicely. When Mollie Bagshaw had her fall the other year, she pressed and pressed the emergency buzzer, but no one came for hours. Turned out Gemma was having her hair done at the time, if you please.

One thing I am grateful for is – don't say too much about this – see, we're not really allowed to keep dogs in here, but for my Skipper, they've done a Nelson – you know, turned a blind eye. I know she doesn't look like much, but she's everything to me. I rescued her; I saved her life.

I just happened to be passing this skip on the Mile End Road and, truth be told, I sometimes look into skips, see, it's a kind of hobby of mine. You never know what you might find in skips (and would I tell?). Well, this time, I says to myself: *That's funny, why is that black bag moving, maybe there's a rat inside*? Then I hear a whimpering sound and I think: *Blimey, there's a dog in there*. And when I finally got her out she just kept staring at me and wiggling her tiny tail.

It was like love at first sight. I was going to call her Skippy, but somehow she became my Skipper. Some bastard had nearly killed her; but that was not her end. For every life saved, there is another life reborn.

One pink ear and one black, she's a Jack; and though she's always been blind in one eye and has a gammy rear leg, she's the brightest little dog you ever did meet. And a better judge of character than I am.

I know they probably say as we walk up and down the Roman Road, most days: *There's Vic the Fish with his mutt, Skipper*. But then, there aren't that many people who know me now. The world has moved on; for better or for worse - I'm not the judge.

I know that Molly Bagshaw doesn't really approve of dogs, and she suspects I've got one. She doesn't like me, anyway. One day, I'm collecting my letters from my pigeon-hole in the rack behind Gemma's office and, unseen, I can hear Molly and Gemma in private conversation. I'll never forget the words I overhear coming from Molly Bagshaw, and they sting me. *I never imagined that I'd have to share a retirement residence with people like Mr Evangelistos*. I've often wondered what she really meant.

Funny, but I don't go down the pub no more. All the old boozers where I used to drink with the lads have gone. Maybe 'cos the lads have gone too. I was in *The Blind Beggar*, a handsome young lad I was, that afternoon that Ronnie shot Georgie Boy from the Richardson Gang. Ronnie was sweet on me. He took me to a party once or twice. I never said nothing about it to the police, mind you. We were like that in them days. But there's nowhere you can go for a quiet pint no more – they're all posh *eateries* and wine bars now.

Say what you like about East Enders, but we love to try new things. I'll do anything once. These days, I like trying out these new cafes, only if they're *dog-friendly*, mind you.

There's a new one half way down the Roman Road. It used to be, years ago, a pie and mash shop, but they've all gone now, almost. Young people just don't like jellied eels. I can't understand it. Can you?

See, the secret of good jellied eels is in the cooking. The jelly comes out of the boil and sets, lovey and sticky, to preserve the eels as long as you like. Makes a lovely little snack, cold. But can you get 'em these days?

This café, it's called *La Rue de Rome.* I think that's French.

Anyway, I go in and I say to the young lady: *Can I bring my dog in here, love?* And I know her: it's Elsie, the Polish girl who used to work in the launderette. And she says, in one of them husky Polish accents: *No problem, my darling, we love well-behaved dogs, and would he like a little water bowl*? Which was nice, even though Skipper is actually a she.

And we settle down at a little table in the corner and then the Polish girl, very pleasant and that, gives me a long list of all the coffees they do, and I say: *Just a normal coffee for me, love, instant's fine*. And she says: *But we don't do instant coffee it's all fresh*; and I say: *Don't worry about it, love, just give me the cheapest one, and I'm sure it'll be very nice*. And she smiles a warm smile and then says, in a way Aunt Leenie used to call *coquette*: *And what about a little pastry with that?*

Surrender. She's got me.

So Skipper and I are sitting nice and quiet in a corner, like, with this filter whatsit and a flaky thingamee reading our *Daily Mail* when, all of a sudden, this huge car – I might say a tank – pulls up outside. It's parked on the pavement right outside the café and then I see a lady - all smartly dressed, ear-rings and beads, and that - open up the hatch at the back, and out comes the most enormous buggy you ever did see, like the lunar module that time the Yanks landed on the moon.

And I watch as she takes a small child from its child-seat at the back and straps the child into the enormous buggy and then manoeuvres the buggy between the tank and the shop front round to the café entrance and pops her head round the door and calls, I suppose to the Polish girl, *Elszbieta! Excuse me but would you mind helping me with my buggy as your entrance is quite absurdly narrow.*

Then there's about three people who get up and help her steer the buggy into the coffee shop, moving tables and rearranging chairs and that, and finally the woman says: *I'll need some cushions and a high chair as I like my daughter to sit at table level with the adults.*

And Elsie the Polish girl runs round her, like it's the Queen of Sheba on a day-out. Quite stressed Elsie was, I think, but still smiling. And there's a lot of kind of apparatus being unbundled and erected and the woman and her little girl, about three to four years old, maybe, settle themselves like a bunch of posh nomads with designer tents in the middle of our East End steppe.

And then the woman says: *We don't need a menu, we know what we want. We come here every Tuesday, and this is our table. The usual, Elszbieta. Quickly, please.*

And there's me and Skipper, looking on from our tiny world at these visitors from far away. The mother looks like one of those mannequins in a fancy shop window but with hair and make-up too; and the daughter looks like a little doll, but not a nice little doll but maybe a bad little doll from one of those German fairy-tales. I could tell that Skipper was perplexed by the way that she kept tugging on her lead.

The little girl was erected in a kind of child's throne from where she chose to gaze at me and Skipper as if we're not supposed to be there.

No, no, no the lady said. *My daughter only takes vegan, gluten-free chocolate. Please remove these noisome objects from our table.*

I must say, I'm not the world's greatest diplomat, but I feel compelled to say*: It's all very nice here, isn't it?* And the lady just stares at me as if I've just farted and then turns to Elsie, the Polish girl - well I call her Elsie, anyway - and says: *We want the gingerbread men with the little bushy beards, as usual...Isn't that right, Jezabelina?* And the little doll-girl half scowls, but then nods.

Well it's none of my business, I say to myself. Takes all sorts. Anyway, I'm thinking I might liven this pastry up with a nice bit of fresh fish since I always carry a goodly morsel of smoked dab or a succulent kipper or a few slices of smoked eel on me in case I feel peckish. So I get out a lovely little portion of grilled haddock what I've wrapped in an hanky and a few choice little smoked anchovies – doesn't do any harm, does it?

And the woman stares at me as if I'd just said something rude, and wrinkles her nose and says in a posh voice to her daughter: *There's a most unpleasant smell in here today, Jezabelina, I do hope it won't bring you out in a rash.*

And I'm really not quite sure what her problem is but it strikes me that my Skipper might be having what I call one of her smelly days. You never know, you see, it's normally the Muslim fellas who object to dogs, though my friend Ali in Stepney loves 'em. He also appreciates a nice kipper too. But that's by-the-by.

So I look across at the lady and I say, all posh, like*: I can assure you, Madam, that my dog is regularly wormed and* *that she is not malodorous*. And at that moment, Elsie brings a tray of gingerbread men, or whatever they are, and the child looks at the confection and begins to blub.

What's wrong Jezabelina?. And the child points towards the plate with a tiny finger and winces.

Elszbieta, this gingerbread man's beard is crumbling. Could you please take it back and bring my daughter a freshly baked one?

Elsie looks peeved but complies and the child stops blubbing, but then the little one fixes me with a gaze and says, suddenly, for all to hear, like a bell chiming through a London fog: *I don't like that man, Mummy*. And everybody in the café looks round, first at the child, and then at me.

Now I never had any children myself but I normally love 'em to bits. I've been godfather to a fair few in my time. But this one, there was something strange about her, and I suddenly felt, well, uncomfortable. So I pat Skipper on the back to reassure her because I know that if I'm not happy, she's not happy, and I get back to my *Daily Mail*.

And then the mother's mobile phone rings and she answers it with *Lady Francesca Poge. Oh, hello darling*...And all this posh chit-chat starts while the daughter looks on. And I see that while the mother is distracted, the child manages to unbuckle herself from her high chair and, in one bound, breaks free and is standing right by my table, staring at me and my Skipper by turns.

To this very day I don't know if that child honestly tried to stroke Skipper or tried, as it seemed to me, to pull her ear; but anyway, Skipper thought she was under attack. Yes, she went for the kid. She bit two little fingers on the kid's right hand right down to the bone.

And there was a general commotion with the kid wailing and screaming a high-pitched scream the like of which I've never heard this side of Hell. And the mother shouting: *Call an ambulance. Call the police.*

It was Elsie who tried to calm things down. I got up to leave with Skipper, having left some cash on the table, and as I get to the door, I hear the woman say: *I'll have that bloody dog put down under the Dangerous Dogs' Act if it's the last thing I do. We shall meet again.*

And I say: *Yes, lady. Greater love hath no man than he lay down his life for his best friend[1].*

But as I'm trotting homewards down Roman Road, I say to Skipper: *Well, the Nazis never got us out; and big money came, yet we stayed while the others fled. But now this lady comes and gets us on the run.*

As I climb into yet another empty bed, all I can say is: *Enough said.*

Autumn

I've had a good life: I never killed no one. I'm truly glad about that.

You don't find many fishmongers round here no more. If you ask me, supermarket fish, all wrapped in plastic, is just not the same at all as lovely fresh fish served on slabs of ice. And what ever happened to John Dory, hake, skate, sprats, turbot and zander? Anchovy balls; poached bass; dogfish, catfish; crawfish – where have they all gone?

---

[1] See Gospel of Saint John, Chapter 15, verses 9-17.

We spent some time down in Margate, me and Skipper.

My old soul mate, Reg Skeggs, moved there years ago when he retired to a nice terraced house not far from Cecil Square. His wife Madge passed away a couple of years ago, poor love. Cancer. So he doesn't mind company.

He's been ringing me for years, saying: *Vic mate, what's wrong with you? Why d'you wanna be cooped up with the wrinklies in Bow when you could be down here in lovely Margate? We've even got culture now, though I wouldn't recommend it myself.*

This time I says: *Reg, mate, I'll be on that fast train from Stratford before you can say mine's a double. See you in the Northern Belle at sundown, mate. One thing: I'm with my partner.*

He says: *Bloody Hell, mate, have you come out at last?* And I says: *Don't be daft mate, I'm coming with Skipper, my Jack.* Pause. Then he says: *That's fine. I don't have nothing against whippets.*

He's still all right, our Reg.

The problem with Reg, though, if truth be told, he's forgotten the goodness of good fish. He thinks a nice fish dinner is deep-frozen then deep-fried battered plaice and oily chips. I tell you, I had to work on him, but he came round soon enough.

The second night I cooked him a right royal fish dinner. I'd picked up some lovely fresh-caught sea bass in Ramsgate harbour. Rub in some sea salt, cut some onion rings, add some bay leaves, thyme and cloves and just bake, basted in butter and lovely, dry white wine (nothing fancy, like Old Floydy would have poured) for about forty five minutes.

Serve with some shiny new boiled potatoes, garnished with parsley. Result: paradise.

Reg eats silently but with gusto. Then, having mopped his plate with a hunk of wholemeal bread, he looks at me in a way I've never seen before. Does he think I'm Madge? I say: *Reg, welcome to the world of Vic the Fish*.

He says to me: *I should have taken up your offer years ago, Vic mate*. I says to him: *It's much too late, mate. You look like an old prune now. But never mind. I'm glad you enjoyed the fish...Anyway: if you like fish you're going to eat like a king as long as I'm around*.

Actually, that was unfair. Reg has got a bit jowly; yet he's kept his tight, Welterweight boxer's body. You can see every muscle, almost. I've seen a lot worse. In fact, he's hardly aged at all, below his neck.

I soon got into this Margate lark, good and proper. It was late autumn but the sun shone brightly every day, rising to a midday peak above the bay. Skipper loved it too, yapping and dancing on the sand each morning. She made some lovely friends, though frankly, down on Margate beach, you don't find dogs of quite her class.

One day Reg and I were boozing in the Northern Belle and this guy comes in with a little tiny white creature, like a bloated mouse on a piece of string. She's got little brown beads for eyes and one half of her little face is white, the other tan. The bloke says: *I'm off to Spain tomorrow for the winter. Anyone want to take care of this pooch*? Reg eyes the dog sagely and her little tail starts wiggling. He says: *I'll take her off you, mate - and don't hurry back from Spain*.

Over a glass of wine later– he's getting very posh, our Reg – he tells me: *I've been waiting for this moment all my life.*

I know that my life has a purpose after all. If life's a game of chance, I'll call her Skittle.

When we get home, the two Jack bitches, after sniffing around one another for a bit, get into the same basket and then fall asleep together. I says to Reg: *Two fat ladies, old and cold, decide to warm one another up*. He replies: *Makes a lot of sense, mate, dunnit*?

One day, we did our little tour of the charity shops, dogs in tow. We headed down the Centre and cast an eye over the tat in the *British Heart Help Centre*, RSPCA Shop and all the rest. Clothes, shoes, prints, knick-knacks, books - all dirt cheap. We came out of *Cancer Care UK*, where Reg bought, for some reason I know not, would you believe it, a 19th century chamber pot for a blueback.

Then Reg goes all funny.

He says to me: *It's him*. I says: *Who's him mate?* He says to me: *Who the Hell do you think I'm bloody talking about?* And I says: *I haven't got a bloody clue mate.* And he says: *I've always known he was still alive*. I'm completely soused, and I says: *How many have you had this morning?*

He shouts: *That old man on the – what d' you call it – the mobility scooter. It's him!*

And he runs and runs up Cecil Street but all I can see is a fat senior accelerating away from a slowing Reg. Then Reg accosts a lady pensioner, saying: *Can I borrow your mobility scooter for five minutes, love?* And she's so bowled over she just smiles. I watch as the two mobility scooters race each other on the hill, but I can see that Reg is lagging as they disappear over the brow. After a few minutes I see disgruntled Reg cruising back and I see him return the scooter to the hapless lady pensioner, defeated and resigned.

One day Reg dragged me to the Turner Museum, or whatever it's called. I says: *You know I don't like art and stuff like that.* And he says: *Just keep your tiny mind open and it might get bigger, like molluscs do.* Reg is the only man who who's ever talked to me like that. And I've always loved the way he speaks. He's always had a kind of class.

There's a huge big sign outside: *Visions: From Raphael to Tracey*.

We reach the entrance – a big atrium, full of light, slightly weird. There's a women who introduces herself as "Tracey" all cooing and lovely to see you, like. She's quite skinny and bit of a fish face (a compliment in my book) but very warm and friendly. She tells us that her Dad had a chippie here in Margate and Reg says: *I think I knew your Dad – wasn't he Mick the Turk?* Yes, I knew the geezer too. She kind of smiles. He turns to me and whispers: *He still owes me a pony – don't say nothing.*

Then Tracey says: *D'you boys want to see my bed? It's here again.* And I say: *That's fine love, but I hope we don't have to pay for the pleasure.* And she says: *It's all right darling, no charge.*

And we walk up this spiral staircase with Tracey wittering, you know, she couldn't have been nicer, but, as for me, I haven't got a clue what she's going on about. Then she presents us with her unmade bed, like in the middle of a bloody spanking new museum.

Well, I says to Reg: *I've seen beds in my time but this nice young lady needs help from Health and Safety.* Reg replies - he was always cleverer - *It's supposed to be a joke, mate.*

Tracey can see that her "bed" doesn't do much for us. So she says: *You don't have to like it darlings, it's just supposed to make you think. We've got some of Turner's greatest work here too – the ones that he painted on the North Kent coast.*

I say: *Look, love, if you want us to sort it out for you, me and Reg here – mind you, he's the tidy one between the two of us - we'll get that duvet sorted at Mo's Launderette quick as you can say "vodka".*

And she says: *You just don't get it, boys, do you? This bed is how I felt at that time – desperate. Have you never felt desperate in your lives? Suppose you could use things around you to express your desperation? Haven't you ever wanted to just shout at the sky? What was your line of work?*

I'm in fish, love, I says. *Always have been, always will be.*

OK, says Tracey, *Let's see what JWMT thought about fish.*

And she steers me, like a rudderless dingy, to a huge canvas, and it takes me minutes to drink it all in. It's a kind of revelation. A vision of another world, but still here: *The New Moon*, 1840.

It is morning, and the locals have gone down to the beach 'cos the fish has come in. There's a bloke running, with some kind of rod over his shoulder. There's two little dogs running towards the waves. There's like a mother with two small children, and she seems upset. The sea is calm and the light is strange. There's something wrong here: I fear a drowning.

I say to Trace: *Someone has perished at sea, is that it?*

She says: *Maybe, but why don't we go inside the painting to find out?*

I says to Reg: *I told you I'd never understand this modern art, mate.* But he gives me a funny look.

Tracey says: *Just hold my hand and we can enter that world if only you believe it is real. Come on, Reg.*

Yes, it's the *Wizard of Oz,* because, in a moment, I feel myself running barefoot on Margate sands, but wearing this funny heavy coat and stiff collar, and I can see Reg, all in twill, up to his knees in the tide, looking out to sea. And Skipper and Skittle are just barking, like dogs bark when they sense unease or danger. And then I turn, and I see Tracey in this weird Victorian garb, clutching the little sobbing urchins and saying through her tears something about Mummy drowning...

Then, I turn towards the way we came and I see a kind of window in the sky, and through this weird window I can see Tracey, and Reg and me, in our normal clothes, looking back towards the sea, but frozen in time, like a painting...

I squeeze Tracey's hand, and I can't help squeezing Reg's with my other hand. And I say: *Let's go back*. And we are back in the gallery, and Tracey is looking at me in a kind of motherly way, as if I was her kid, and she wants to comfort me.

And then, she says: *And look at this one over here. That's fish for you. It's called The Miraculous Draft of Fishes, by Raphael, and it was painted in the early sixteenth century. It's actually what they call a cartoon – like a sketch – for a pope. It's owned by the Queen, so aren't we lucky to look at it? What do you think, boys?*

It's a bit weird really 'cos there's two ecstatic blokes with beards saying thank you to a cool, laid-back geezer, sitting in boat, as two lads unload fish from a second boat, three greedy black cormorants looking on.

Reg says: *Those muscly geezers in the background look like boys I know who work out at MuscleWorks Gym in Bethnal Green.*

Tracey replies: *Darling, you've confirmed everything I learnt at art school. I owe you one.*

Then some slight bloke with a clipboard comes sidling up to Trace and says: *Tracey, darling, Will Gompertz of the BBC has been waiting, like twenty-five minutes, and he's got to get back to London on the fast train for cocktails at the Royal Academy. Don't please miss this one, darling - it matters.*

Tell him, I'll meet him by my bed and he can get anything he needs, she says to the clipboard. Then, she turns to us and says: *Boys, it's been a very great pleasure. Come and see me in Spitalfields. Here's my card.*

Say what you like about that Gemma, but she did me one big turn. One morning I've just got back from the fish market with a lovely fresh skate what I'm going to make into a nice spread with lemon and chilli, and the bloody phone rings.

Oh Vic, she says in that silly little girl's voice, *I know you've been worried and you don't have to worry any more*. And I says: *What have you got to tell me, love?*

And she tells me that some kind of inspector has been round, further to a complaint about a dog, wanting to search my flat. So Gemma lets them in, shows them round, and sends them away with a flea in their ear, 'cos *there ain't no dog*. It then turns out she's hidden all Skipper's dog beds and toys and had cleaned up my flat, which, if truth be told, probably smells mostly of fish, but there you are. She's a sweet girl, really.

Then she tells me something strange, unexpected. She says I'd be better off staying indoors 'cos winter's coming early this year, and with a vengeance. Something about an *Arctic Inversion*. Whatever that is. What will they think of next? I says to myself, to scare pensioners?

Next morning, Reg receives a letter, and goes all quiet, like.

I don't want to hurt him but I feel I have to go. Later that morning, I says to Reg: *Reg Mate, it's been great but it's time for me and Skipper to get back to Smoke for the winter. But, if it's all the same to you, we'll be back in the spring.*

And he looks back at me, sad, almost forlorn. But he walks us back to the station, carrying my Stanley bag. Then he says to me: *I've got debts, Vic. About fifty grand. The house is gonna have to go, mate. But I'm glad you enjoyed it for a few weeks. It meant a lot to me.*

What are you talking about, mate, I ask my friend*, you had a pension, right?*

It's all gone, mate. Started with Madge's funeral. She wanted plumed horses, big flowers, suites at the Sands Hotel for mourners, a marble tombstone the size of a small car. You know. I never did recover, financially. So I backed a few gee-gees to get the money back and, one thing led to another...

I don't think I do wanna know mate...

He even stands on the platform as the High Speed train begins to accelerate (high pitch whistle) out of the station. He might even have been crying. And just at that moment, it begins to snow.

As that fast train speeds across Kent towards Canterbury I can see the fields getting whiter.

Blimey, I says to Skipper: *We're gonna have a white Christmas, at last.*

Winter

Three weeks it was, three weeks of constant snow and growing icicles. If Hell was hot, the East End was the coldest place alive. Molly Bagshaw slipped on the ice on the first day – never walked again, poor love. She doesn't go out no more. Poor cow.

Gemma kept pushing notes under our doors with the gist of: *Residents are advised not to go during the extreme winter weather conditions.* And then, one day: *Please stay in your rooms today as there no one is available to assist you during The Emergency.* And then, a few days later, a note which read: *Due to extreme weather conditions the Christmas Party has been cancelled. An emergency Christmas pack will be delivered to your flat soon.*

Bugger that, I said to Skipper that morning. We need our walk, as ever. And we headed off through the drifts towards the Park.

Victoria Park, known to all true East Enders as *Vicky Park*, is the most beautiful park in the world; spring, summer, autumn, winter; lakes with islands, bandstands, trees and flowers. It lies on ley lines that even the Romans would not disturb, for fear of infamy, that's why they built their road to Colchester where they did. It doesn't matter what goes on, it just remains the loveliest oasis in that terrible desert called London. In summer, everyone makes love there, one way or another: dogs, ducks, boys and girls; and only the trees bide their modesty.

By the time we got there, Skipper and I beheld a snow-scape, shimmering in the morning sun. And we head, as we always do, towards the lake, which is frozen solid as I haven't seen it since the long winter of 1962-63, when whole parts of England were cut off by snow drifts for months on end.

And to my surprise, though the roads are deathly quiet on account of the *extreme conditions*, I see that around the pavilion that used to be the old coffee shop, there's a kind of car park of huge gleaming four-by-fours; some black some white; their tyres all bound by shining silver chains (expensive no doubt), parked casually on the corner of Vicky Park Road. Then I see that, though the park is chill and quiet, the pavilion is open for lunch, and it looks like the posh mums have come in force, their kids in tow.

I can't help wanting to peep at the menu outside the pavilion, just to see if there are any decent, affordable fish dinners going, not that I'm desperate 'cos I've still got a pocket full of lovely fish treats. And as I get there, crunching through powdery snow which Skipper loves to sniff, I behold a sign that this lovely old Victorian pavilion is no longer the pavilion at all. It's been taken over by *New Management*

As I get nearer I see that the old coffee shop has a new name. It's now called *Pomodoro.* The roof always looked a bit like a bloody tomato to me, so I don't know why they call it by something foreign. Anyway, I read the menu, even though some foreign-looking geezer stares through the glass from the warmth inside at me and my shivering Skipper outside.

I read: *Warm the Cockles Menu: Sea bream steamed in a Martini and fennel mist, served with crushed pumpkin seeds, honey and digestive biscuit drizzle, potato and mountain pumpkin hash browns, on a bed of clarified, chopped celeriac.* And at the price of a day trip to Margate - with all the trimmings. (The Margate trip, that is).

Bloody hell, I says to Skipper: *What's the need to mess around with lovely, fresh sea bream? These people don't know nothing.*

So we – me and Skipper – find a little quiet seat, with a lovely view of Pagoda Island, and take out a nice little firm chunk of jellied eel what I've prepared myself the day before. See, the thing about nibbles is that they keep you nice and warm.

And I nibble, sharing with Skip, of course. And as I'm sitting there quietly with Skipper, I observe a strange procession of four tiny little beautiful winged angels with ice skates on their feet. And they start to play stringed instruments – tiny harps – and blow on whistles. So getting behind a tree with Skittle, I watch events unfold.

And the angels launch themselves upon the lake with the grinding, scratching sound of metal upon ice, like tiny vibrant dolls, pigtails flapping in the glacial breeze, giggling excitedly with all the natural hilarity of little girls together. And there they go, all in a line, skating towards Pagoda Island, as if in seventh heaven.

Then a woman appears by the lake, all worried, like. She calls: *Jezabelina, Trixabel, Jocasta, Araminta - Come back!*

Four little horses; one Apocalypse.

I can see that they are skating in a formal pattern as if they had all planed it themselves to please their mums. But now the mums are all outside calling: *Come Back.* Of course there is nothing much that they can do but wail. We see the little girls reach Pagoda Island and then turn back. And as they glide across the ice like tiny creatures in a fairy tale, there is the ugly sound of cracking ice, a sound you never want to hear. And I, Skipper and the assembled Mums can see a child swallowed by the lake.

The mother screams. I know now that it's that woman in the café who wanted my Skipper put down – but that's all, like, behind us, because I have to help. Then I see the lady running across the ice. I shout: *Be careful, lady.*

There's a man who's come out of the café and he's sort of carrying a rope. And I decide that Skip and I might best be of help if we can get to the bridge between the foreshore and the island. I grab the rope and run. Skip follows me, apace.

By the time I get to the bridge the mother has almost reached the gaping hole in the ice where the daughter disappeared. I can hear a searing, childish moan. I say to Skip, *Go onto the ice, I'll throw the rope from the bridge*. And, eyeing me with those bright, deep little eyes, I think she understands me.

She tears across the ice and then stops to watch me gain the bridge. The mother is almost at the ice hole now; and then it happens. The mother vanishes beneath the ice in a sort of explosion of sugar.

I shout to Skip: *Go to the little girl.* Once more she understands. There is a tiny hand above the ice hole, wrapped in a kind of frilly cuff. Skipper finds the cuff and pulls at it with all the persistence of a terrier. The lifeless body of a little girl soon slides across this ice. What can a man do? I tie the rope around my waist and lower myself over the bridge. It's just twenty metres to the little girl but I figure that, if I can reach her, I can haul us both back up to the bridge, maybe given help. I say to Skipper: *Home girl.* And she knows her job is done.

When I reach the tiny little thing she's like a rag doll. I have no idea if she's still alive. I don't even think of the mother at this point. But I grab her with my stronger left hand and haul on the rope with my right. By the time we regain the bridge there is a small crowd of helpers. I see the agonised face of my friend, Ali, who reaches down with strong arms to propel me the last two metres onto the bridge.

She isn't breathing. Now I know, as a fish lover, my breath may sometimes smell, but I had the deepest sense that this kid wanted to live. I pressed my lips to hers and gave her the full content of my lungs. Nothing. There was a stirring around me. Someone said: *Help is coming.* Help too late is not help at all, thought I. I tried again, and this time I was conscious that Skipper was beside me. She'd got back alright.

I blows and blows. The crowd goes quiet. I think of my poor mother and dear Aunt Leenie. I try to fathom the meaning of their lives, as I often do. And I look up, and there they both are, though I only remember my Mum's face from Leenie's photos. They are smiling at me and I hear my mother say: *Go on, son, you can do it.*

I breathe hard into this limp child's mouth and pound her chest, as many times as I can. It seems like eternity, and yet no time at all. Beyond time. A place beyond suffering.

And then the child splutters, and twitches, and, yes, breathes. Fitfully at first. But she is alive. No sooner have I grasped this fact than the uniformed paramedics arrive, saying: *Move over, mate, leave this to the experts.*

All I can remember is me and Skip walking home through the snow-scape accompanied by the sound of police sirens and whirling helicopters. That night, after a hot shower, as I sat in my favourite chair, with Skipper curled up on my lap, someone called me from a newspaper. I can't remember what I said. The next morning, I read something in the Daily Mail along the lines of *Celebrity mother perishes in ice tragedy while daughter is saved by local fishmonger…Society hostess, Lady Francesca Poge, died yesterday in a horrific accident in Victoria Park, East London…* It was all too much to take in.

Gemma was still off because she couldn't catch her train. We residents were delivered *utility boxes* by bored-looking men in high-viz jackets. This was going to be a rotten Christmas.

But early on Christmas Eve morning, the postman turns up – the first post for a week or more. Nothing for Molly Bagshaw, I see. I checks my pigeon hole. A letter. Could this be a Christmas card from Reg? Naah. Shame does that to a man. I took the letter back to my flat and told Skip: *Don't worry girl, at least we've got each other.*

So I open the letter and I realise that it *is* a Christmas card. *The Poge Trust wishes you a Merry Christmas. What's all that all about?* I ask Skipper. Then I notice that there is a letter enclosed. All printed out on *Poge Trust* notepaper. *What do they want with me?*

Dear Mr Evangelistos, on behalf of the Poge Trust, we think it appropriate to rectify an administrative error that may have been made in 1988 (although no liability is admitted) when you applied for a stall in New Billingsgate Market, and were declined. We are happy to enclose a cheque by way of compensation…

Then I notice there's like a spidery child's handwriting along the bottom of the Christmas Card. *Thank you for saving my life. Jezebelina xxx.* I says to Skipper: *Poor little mite, she's lost her Mum, like us.*

And then it fell to the floor. A cheque. Skipper jumped down to pick it up. *Careful, Skip*, I said. I grabbed it before she might do what Jacks do.

I read it. One hundred thousand fucking pounds. I felt stunned. Bite me, Skip, I said. But she just stared at me like I was a nutter. And then I got her message.

Yes, of course I know what to do, Skip, I said. Get your boots on.

See, me, I never had no bank account. Why would you want to give your cash to strangers when you could keep it in your pocket? I knew what to do.

Skip and I got decked out in our finest, and with the biggest bag we could, we headed down the Roman Road. First stop: Barclays Bank.

No, I know I haven't got a bank account, love, that's why I want to put this in my mate's bank account, cos' I always used to bank his wages for him. Is there a problem, darling? And one more thing, would you mind giving the gentleman a ring to tell him his balance. I expect he'll be upgraded to Superior Customer status now.

Then we got a taxi through the snow to Stratford International and I bought a one-way ticket to Margate. Small dogs go free. I texted Reg to say that I'd see him shortly.

When the train stopped at Margate after dusk I could see Reg and Skittle on the platform, looking awkward.

He met me and Skip in silence, like he'd lost his voice. Then, as we walked past Dreamland through the ice, he turned to me and said: *I don't know if you won the lottery, mate, but I can't take it. It wouldn't be right.*

We walked on, still in silence, the question hanging over us, and made our way to *The Belle* where Maisie the barmaid greeted us. *Well, if it isn't my favourite pair of gentleman*, she said.

We got drinks, then I asked him: *Why wouldn't it be right?* And he says: *It's not like we're a married couple, is it?*

And I was surprised by my reply, cos' I hadn't planned it. I says: Well, that's allowed now, isn't it? That might be a nice way to spend our final years.

And Reg stands up and looks at me: *Is that a proposal, mate?*

Yes, I says. And we're standing face to face and I can see little tears rolling down his cheeks. And we just grab one another, in a kind of bear hug.

I've always loved you, I choked. *It hurt so much at times.*

I know mate, and the silly thing is I've always loved you. Madge always knew it, she used to tease me about it. You were my first love – and now my last. I accept.

And then Maisie, who has overheard all this: *Sounds like Champagne is called for*. And with that the entire pub gives us a cheer.

Later that evening we went to midnight mass at Saint Mildred's and there's the lovely lady vicar standing outside to greet the people. Someone from the pub said jokily, *Meet the happy couple*. And the vicar says: *You are very welcome, boys. I'm not supposed to do this officially, but come to the altar during the service and I'll bless your union.*

We walked back to Reg's, slow snowflakes settling on the dogs' backs. That Christmas night I felt that something yearned for over so many years had been granted at last. You see: my *record* all them years ago came about just because I practiced the wrong kind of love. It all seems silly now.

Skipper and Skittle are still sharing baskets too.

It's been a lovely chin-wag, even though poor old Reg here didn't get a word in edge-ways, but there you are. Yes, mate, of course I can tell you what happened the following spring, though you should always be careful of endings.

Spring

See, with the money left over, we bought a ketch. We were fishermen now. During winter's end we painted and repaired her. Then, one day, just after Easter, Reg said: *Let's go fishing.* And we did.

We set off by night and headed to Foreland Point, with Skipper and Skittle aboard. We caught nothing that night, not a sprat, not a mackerel. But as we tacked back to Margate marina in the early morning light we ran across a sand bank. And, blow me, there's a big geezer standing on the bank and he stares at us as if he's been expecting us, caught in a shaft of sunlight.

The geezer calls out to us: *Have you caught anything? No*, says Reg. And the geezer shouts back: *Throw your net out to the right*. And we do just what he said; we drop the net, as if we were boys again. And, you won't believe it, but the net fills up with so many cod that we can't even manage between the two us to haul it in again. Reg and I look at one another, and Reg cries out: *It's him – it's Tubby!* And, then at last I realise that it is old Tubby Isaacs himself.

Well now, Reg can't contain himself with surprise and joy and he just dives into the wine-dark water, stark bollock-naked, and swims like crazy towards the sand bank, with Skipper and Skittle looking on, amazed.

I manoeuvre the ketch ashore to find Reg with Tubby who's cutting fresh loaves of bread and he's got a charcoal barbeque going and he's grilling fish in the early morning sunshine. And Tubby just looks at me as if he's never been away and he says: *Bring me some of that fish you've just caught*. And Reg somehow manages to drag the net ashore. *One hundred and fifty three*, he says.

And Tubby just calmly says: *Let's have breakfast*. And he serves us both a hunk of the most beautiful bread with lovely, fresh delicious chunks of cod just cooked lightly with sea salt and lemon. And of course there's enough for Skipper and Skittle who bark and dance upon the silver sand, and then lick Tubby's feet to bits.

And if that was the best fish dinner I've ever had with Reg and the mutts, thanks to Tubby, I know that there'll be many more to come.

The Theatre of Ghosts

Indeed it was I who played Prospero that season, ruler of the Enchanted Isle. I, Aubrey Simpkins, *actor*. The theatre is in my blood. I was born and bred on these boards. My mother and my father were both jobbing Thespians. I was conceived -so my mother told me just before she died in a cloud Gauloise, *Chanel* and gin - *entre acte*, during a production of *Aladdin* at the Empire Theatre, Harrogate. She never revealed, though, quite who my father was.

One becomes a master of one's craft by practice. I learnt much more from dear Larry than from RADA, my dears. I once said to Larry: *Master* (for we always called him The Master), *Just for a short moment be Archie Rice*. And suddenly, I was in the presence of Archie, *The Entertainer*, even though Larry never even said a word – it was the way he looked at me, how he held himself. It was uncanny. And then we would say: *Master, be Henry V*. And I would be sipping in the company of the young King.

Of course, I was never in his league. But I have hardly ever been out of work. Except when that silly sitcom folded on ITV and we were all sent packing. But I was soon back on the road, in rep. Darlings, of course I relish panto. In my youth I made an athletic Jack (as in Beanstalk); and these days, yes, some years, I'll be an ugly sister. I don't mind at all. I just cannot abide a day without the smell of greasepaint and the glare of footlights.

You are quite right that most theatres are haunted. Most of them pullulate with ghosts. We actors can sometimes hear the echoes of long forgotten laughter in empty stalls; the resonant murmur of applause afforded to dead colleagues after the house has emptied; the cries of "bravo" and "encore" from first nights long ago. But there was one theatre, my dears, which was notorious for spectral encounters and - that is where I wish to take you for my tale.

The Priory Theatre, Dartford, is one of the most mysterious theatres in England. In fact, many actors deny that it exists at all, though I can assure you that it does. No, no, dear boy, nothing to do with that modern carbuncle, the Orchard Theatre, which attracts less affluent Darfordians – we try to avoid that one if we can. No, the Priory Theatre is nestled in an alley way behind Holy Trinity Church in what remains of the medieval town. Even very few locals know that it's there.

I grant you, Dartford is a funny place. Its burghers seem these days to perambulate around its High Street like waifs who have lost something precious which they know they shall never regain. The planners have constructed a *ring road*, obliterating most of the old priory walls, which motorists pursue in concentric circles, as if driving pointlessly towards nowhere. But at least, the Bard is not forgotten there.

Old Bernard, the caretaker and general factotum at the Priory Theatre once told me that he regularly saw the figure of a hooded monk on the stage late at night. Several times he had accosted him, but the spectral figure just turned and vanished. Mind you, Old Bernard was often on the sauce. But it was on my first night as Prospero in Lester Benning's 1999 production of the Bard's last play that I knew that something ghostly was afoot.

Theatre-lovers of the English-speaking world will know that Lester is notorious for his left-wing slant. It was only after I was auditioned for the part that, over an extended lunch in Sheekey's, Lester told me of his concept. He explained, over several bottles of Bollinger, that essentially, William of Stratford had concocted, in is swansong, an incisive critique of imperialism and neo-colonialism. I, as Prospero, represented colonial aggression against *first-nation peoples*. Therefore, he would translate the magical fable to the late 19th Century. I would be wearing a monocle, pith helmet and handlebar moustaches. Miranda (poor girl – she had not at this late juncture yet been cast) would be presented as the scarred, damaged victim of my (Prospero's) inherent patriarchal violence. By dint of egregious make-up, Miranda would display more bruises than a ripe peach.

I must say that I was not terribly convinced by this interpretation of one of the finest works in all literature; but, alas, I had just been blacklisted by commercial television and I would have done anything to get my name back on the programme sheets. One must remember that Lester, in those days, was still unassailable. He was lauded across *Theatre-land* as the hero who had been the first man to say the F-word on television; and he had once famously urinated through the letterbox of the South African Embassy. No one could gainsay Lester then.

The night before first night I was applying my makeup and faux moustaches for the final dress rehearsal and turned towards the mirror to behold the old magus that I had become. And what stared back at me was not my face, nor even that of the magician himself, but another, unfamiliar, though *actorly,* face - which wore an expression of pained disdain. I froze. I closed my eyes. And when I opened them again I beheld my Prospero's whiskered mask.

It was only after the dress rehearsal, at a reception to which Lester had invited some local dignitaries and Labour

Party bigwigs in the theatre bar, that I noticed the portrait of the legendary actor, Sir Adrian Bates (1893-1944). His countenance was precisely the one that I had encountered in the mirror some two hours earlier. For a second time that evening, I froze.

Then Lester approached me, possibly sensing that I was disturbed.

Ah, he said, *you know what happened to poor old Sir Adrian Bates. It was in August 1944, towards the end of the War. The Germans were pummelling London and Kent with flying bombs. He was playing Prospero here, that night. Very sadly, the theatre took a direct hit – on the stage itself. Most of the cast and audience survived but poor Adrian and Dame Cecilia Raven, who was playing Miranda - though she must have been about 60 by then - were blown to pieces. Tragic business. There's a small plaque to their memory in the Abbey.*

I must say Lester did not seem too perturbed by this forgotten theatrical tragedy; but what he told me chilled my spine, the more so since this tragedy had occurred in the very month of my birth.

When I returned to my dressing room I found my possessions in disarray. It should be said that fine actors always bring a collection of time-tested mascots and charms. The ladies of our profession are consumed these days by cuddly toys – mostly unsightly bears. We actors of a certain tradition prefer artefacts of Thespian association. For example, I never go anywhere without a small lacquer framed portrait of Edmund Kean, a Lalique decanter once owned by Oscar Wilde (filled of course with good gin), and that splendid ebony walking cane that Larry gave me near his end. He said, in a gravelly voice: *You might need this one day, old boy: it is of no further use to me*.

Well, all of these precious objects had been displaced. But not necessarily by ghosts. Rather by the last-minute Miranda who had been parachuted in, thanks to Lester's lack of casting skills.

Renata Zullenblacker was a young American actress whose fame had preceded her arrival in England in the form of a popular but entirely vulgar film entitled *How Girls Have Fun.* I've never seen it myself but apparently it consists mostly of gratuitous nudity. I, personally, found her brooding and sullen.

Hi, Aubrey, she offered as I entered my dressing room. *I hope you don't mind my using your dressing room, but something really spooky just happened. I returned to my dressing room to change and the mirror on the wall crashed to the floor. I mean, there's like shards of glass everywhere. That Bernard guy is clearing up for me. But I just couldn't wait to get these purple marks off my face...*

Where is my stick, Renata? But she just ignored me.

What was really kind of weird was that, as I stood there, I felt like the presence of a lady and a hand seemed to reach out and touch my hair. I just freaked out.

I left my ebony walking stick beside the dressing table, Renata. It appears to have been moved. It has a silver handle engraved with the initials LO.

Is it valuable?

Probably. But its value to me is inestimable. It was a gift from one of the great masters of our art.

This exchange left me exasperated. Happily, Old Bernard later found my cherished walking stick inside the gentleman's facility, stage left. It was never resolved how it got there. It was only later that I learned that Larry had often worked with Sir Adrian Bates.

But it was on the first night that the ghostly manifestations appeared on stage. I had just begun my torture of the *abhorred slave*, Caliban. Now Caliban was played by the then upcoming young black British actor, Kwame Odinga-Jones. Kwame would later make his name as the first black Hamlet in another of Lester's West End productions, but back then he was little known. He hailed, like Burton, Hopkins and Sheen from a Welsh valley just inland from Port Talbot and he spoke with the rugged, songful intonation of a son of the valleys. Personally, I couldn't understand a word; but Lester was keen that he should retain his "authentic" manner of speech.

Caliban was to enter from stage right, whereupon my Prospero was supposed to thrash him mercilessly with a cane for a good minute. For protection, Kwame was equipped with a cushion in his doublet which afforded him the gait of a hunchback of which even Richard III would be proud. After the dress rehearsal, Lester had scolded me for having thrashed Kwame with insufficient vigour. *Remember,* he had said*, you're a detestable bastard – make that audience hate you...* And at the last minute before first night Lester had instructed that Caliban-Kwame wear cricket pads so that I could kick him in the shins as well.

So there I was stage-central, scowling through my moustaches at the audience, despatching my *tricksy spirit* Ariel, who, by the way was played by the delicious Miss Petronella Steam (the love of my life for many years thereafter, as readers of the tabloid press will know). And, as Caliban-Kwame enters, I offer a blood-curdling *Thou poisonous slave, got by the devil himself* and then begin the vicious assault.

But as I am administering a vigorous thrashing to the unfortunate Caliban I become aware of another actor on stage, just behind me and to the right, who should not be there. Cane held aloft as if about to bring down another blow, I turn to the figure and say the next line as if to him: *Upon thy wicked dam, come forth!*

Now old professionals can feel an audience even when they cannot see them through the glare of footlights. One almost instinctively knows their mood. An untimely cough; contagious fidgeting, inappropriate whispers; and – worst of all – the faint titter of shared ridicule – these are all things that a true actor senses instantly. On this occasion, I felt the sudden concentrated hush of an expectant audience uncertain of whether they are in the presence of greatness or bathos. It is a moment that I have experienced only two or three times.

And then I beheld the face of my spectral co-star. Of course, it was that of Sir Adrian Bates, wearing an expression of sardonic disapproval. He seemed to be saying *Never mind, young chap; you'll get the hang of it...*

Kwame, who as I have already said, has abundant talent, sensed my change of mood, my strange distraction, and acted up to it. *A south-west blow on ye, and blister ye all o'er...*was uttered with a touch of tenderness that suggested that he, Kwame-Caliban, was in control - and that it was I, Aubrey-Prospero who was lost.

The rest of the performance played out much as the final dress rehearsal except that I noticed that Renata's Miranda seemed strangely distracted and distant in the final scene with Ferdinand. *How beauteous mankind is! Oh brave new world that has such people in it!* These words were uttered as if from another world.

Then, at the end of the play I launched into Prospero's epilogue: *Now my charms are all o'erthrown*...And it was during the final two lines of the play that Adrian's ghost re-appeared and proceeded to upstage me.

As you from crimes would pardoned be/ Let your indulgence set me free.

A tumultuous applause unfurled but, try as I might, I could not take my bow because there was Ghost Adrian immediately in front of me, bowing and blowing kisses and making elaborately courteous hand gestures of appreciation in the manner of seasoned actors of the older generation, flailing his hat through the air and doing a little skip of a man preparing for his fourth curtain call. I turned and walked off stage, only to bump straight into Lester who looked cross.

What are you doing, man? They loved it. Get back on stage and take your bow...

The next day the notices were mixed. The *Daily Mail* had sent Cedric Snipe - motoring him down to Dartford especially on account of my leading role. Snipe is a critic who has always caused me trouble. In fact, we cordially loathe one another. Yes, it is true that I once hurled the contents of my champagne glass in his face at a soirée in Chelsea. The man is odious and shallow; no doubt like many of his readers.

I had chosen to stay in the Bull Hotel in Dartford High Street rather than return each night to my flat in Maida Vale – the one I inherited from my late mother. The chatelaine of that commodious establishment, one Mrs Plender, was herself an amateur dramatist who had recently played Mrs Bennet in a local adaptation of *Pride and Prejudice*, and was in awe of anyone who trod the stage for a living. In fact, her manner was, if anything, a little overly enthusiastic and attentive. She kept assuring me that she would be a model of discretion if any gentlemen of the press came prowling, and that she was *au fait* with the needs and foibles of professional actors.

Over breakfast, which Mrs Plender insisted on cooking for me personally, I chanced upon a copy of the *Daily Mail* on the newspaper rack and returned to my seat at which I knew I would soon be lavished by Mrs Plender's solicitous attentions. As I sat down I could not help but notice a caption on the top right corner of the front page: *Has Aubrey Simpkins got Alzheimers? Turn to Page 23.*

I wouldn't go reading that nonsense, Mr Aubrey, Sir. There was a very favourable review of last night's performance in the Dartford Echo, this morning. We Dartfordians can tell quality when we see it...

But I had already turned to page 23. I read:

Last night Aubrey Simpkins, who readers will recall played the hapless Russell Mullet in the failed ITV sitcom about a bunch of n'er-do-well gravediggers, "For Whom the Bell Doesn't Toll", played Prospero in William Shakespeare's farewell play, The Tempest, at the cosy Priory Theatre Dartford. Simpkins ludicrously dressed in Lester Benning's production as a 19th century colonial apparatchik wielding a cane, seemed every so often to literally lose the plot. At one point he started ranting to a non-existent member of the cast. At the end of the play he just walked off the stage, refusing to take the initial bow. Now the question is: did Mr Benning intend that Mr Simpkins play the role of the magus as a man afflicted by dementia? Or – more plausibly perhaps – is Mr Simpkins really showing signs of developing dementia in real life? My sources tell me that the latter is more likely...On the other hand, the delightful Ms Renata

Zullenblacker, a Hollywood starlet making her debut on the English stage, was a triumphant Miranda...

And so the nonsense continued over two entire columns. I am afraid that Mrs Plender's excellent kippers went untouched.

Lester had returned to London after the first night and so I chose to spend the morning of the second productively. I visited Dartford's splendid neo-Palladian library, which stands in a corner of that town's justly famous botanical gardens. When on tour I always take the opportunity to read in the mornings before a sound sleep in the afternoon. My favourite reading has, as I am sure you will have guessed, a theatrical flavour. I am probably one of England's leading experts on the history of our theatre and have indeed lectured on the subject in America. And it is greatly to Dartford library's credit that it has an entire corner dedicated to the history of our national passion.

I have often reflected on the power of chance that the first book that I pulled down from a high shelf was – so I discovered – a fat volume entitled *Chance Life: The Life and Times of Dame Cecelia Raven* by one Sebastian Moncrieff. Surely, was it even more improbable that then I opened the book in the centre to behold a photo plate which immediately arrested me.

Sir Adrian Bates as Widow Twankey, and Dame Cecilia as Aladdin in a production of Aladdin, Empire Theatre Harrogate, Christmas 1943. Miss Hermione Simpkins, on Sir Adrian's right, plays Princess Jasmine.

My mother. My beloved mother. Well, actually, I do admit that my mother could be somewhat trying at times; but it was glorious to see that her long career had been remembered in this unexpected photograph. For a brief moment, I felt quite elated. But then I thought it was curious that my mother had never mentioned that she had worked with the illustrious Sir Adrian and Dame Cecilia. How unexpected life can be; even at the age of fifty-five.

That evening of the second night, I entered my dressing room early – there is something about second nights that always surprises and I am nothing if not prepared for adversity. It was indeed an early summer's evening and I was arrested by the sunshine beating through the drapes onto my mirror. But as soon as I entered the room I noted that my (Oscar's) Lalique decanter had been moved. And – more worryingly – its crystal stopper had been removed completely.

Suddenly, there was some kind of power cut and all the lights around my mirror went out. Then I smelt – in this order – a waft of expensive French perfume and the strong essence of pungent continental cigarettes. Gauloise!

Mother, I asked the air, *are you here?* Of course I expected no reply until it came.

*Aubrey, darling. Mmmw, mwmm...*The ghost of my resplendent mother kissed the air just before my cheeks. I could not help but notice that she appeared to be wearing a wedding dress and carried her veil in her right hand.

My, my darling how wonderful...But how stout you have become...

I beg your pardon, dear mother...?

Don't be obtuse, Aubrey. You were always a greedy boy and I told you in adolescence that if you did not curb your appetites you would become plump...

No as a general rule one should never be uncivil to ghosts, especially if the ghost in question is that of one's mother. But these comments about my girth annoyed me grievously.

Well, mother. I think it ill behoves you to lecture me on the virtues of moderation. After you died it took me a week to remove all the empty gin bottles from your flat in Maida Vale...

That is quite enough, Aubrey. You will never understand what I went through all those years – and how much sympathy did you ever have for me? I sent you to a minor public school with a theatrical tradition – and do you know how I ever paid your school fees...?

No Mother, I don't know. And surely, you have not come back to tell me. Why, indeed have you come to see me?

Darling, Aubrey – I did not come here to see you. I am looking for your father...

And then, as ghosts sometimes do, she turned and walked right through the wall. I was about to call for help when Old Bernard entered the room excitedly.

Mr Aubrey, he said, are you all right, sir? I heard you shouting.

If I tell you what I have just seen, my dear Bernard, you would think me quite mad.

Not at all, sir. If you have seen what I see every night, sir, you might say like Prince Hamlet that there are more things in Heaven and Earth than exist in your philosophy, Horatio.

Good old Bernard.

I said: *Bernard, there is something ghostly afoot in this theatre.*

He replied: *Tell me about it, Sir. Last night Miss Renata claims she saw the ghost of an actress on stage in her final scene...*

He left sometime later, after several gins.

Adrian's ghost appeared to me again that second night but, as I had been half expecting him, he was not able to discommode me as on the first. I was able to thrash Kwame with easy felicity. At the play's conclusion, the ghost tried once again to upstage my curtain call with another elaborate display of bowing. But I just ignored him and took my curtain call at his side. An actor must never allow anything to come between him and his public.

Back at the Bull Hotel, Mrs Plender had most thoughtfully left refreshment in my room in the form of a bottle of gin and another of vermouth with a courteous note saying how pleased she was to have an actor of my standing and reputation at her establishment. I was able to mix an excellent and copious dry Martini. I was not tired enough to sleep but instead began to peruse the library book about the golden age of English theatre in which Dame Cecelia Raven had loomed so large.

It seems that Dame Cecelia and Sir Adrian had had a long-standing affair early on in their careers, but that he in middle age had taken up with younger women, something that had greatly perturbed her. By the time that their lives were so brutally terminated by the Nazi missile, they were legends of the stage, but few people realised that relations between them were so strained that they hardly spoke. The writer, the aforementioned Moncrieff, speculated that Sir Adrian was in a relationship with a much younger woman at the time of his death.

At breakfast the next morning I could not help noticing that the odious man Snipe had again been scribbling his torpid prose for the *Daily Mail*. In his *Theatrical Whispers* column he predicted that the *Tempest's* run in Dartford may have to be brought to a premature close. He related that Renata Zullenblacker had told *Variety* magazine that her English theatrical debut was "weird". Once again I left a pair of perfectly fine kippers quite untouched, much to Mrs Plender's chagrin.

That morning I was possessed of an unusual disquiet. I could not help thinking about my mother's mysterious appearance in my dressing room the day before. Of course, that apparition was almost certainly the product of my own unconscious mind. But what did it all mean? I was struck by the notion that there was some kind of mystery concerning my own origins, the nature of which I was condemned to unravel.

I went to the theatre early and immediately accosted dear Old Bernard in the monk-like cell he generally inhabited beneath the stage. It is a kind of Aladdin's cave, full of obscure theatrical artefacts and various forms of bric-a-brac. The leather gloves once word by Dame Edith Evan's when playing Lady Bracknell in *The Importance of Being Earnest*; a top hat used by Albert Finney in a production of *Nicholas Nickleby*: these are just two of the unremarkable yet magical objects with which old Bernard surrounds himself.

Bernard, I said, as I understand it, at the time that the theatre was bombed in the War, it was owned by the legendary impresario, Connie Lennox...

Oh yes, Mr Aubrey, Sir, I knew him well. Such a fine and kindly gentleman. Everyone called him "Bunny". He was the one who recruited me to this theatre as an errand boy when I was just fourteen years old. And I'm still here, Mr Aubrey, some sixty five years later. I'm part of the furniture here you might say. Would you care for a macaroon, Sir...?

Thank you, dear Bernard, but I have been most adequately provisioned by the excellent Mrs Plender... Sixty five years, you say. Then you were here during the War – when the theatre was bombed..?

Oh, Mr Aubrey, I remember it like it was yesterday. I remember that moment when the doodlebug engine cut out and then the thirty seconds of silence while the matinee performance just continued – and then the horrific bang and me being thrown to the floor as if by an evil wind – and the dust and the screaming and the acrid smell of burning mortar. That was the worst day of my life, Mr Aubrey. And poor dear Sir Adrian and poor, Dame Cecelia met their end just as the Bard's las play was about to end...

My God, Bernard, I had no idea that you were there then. Was Connie present at the time?

Oh yes. It was said at the time that Mr Lennox was due to go to a wedding that day at the church next door, Holy Trinity. The wedding was to have been held between the matinee and the evening performance and several members of the cast were to have attended. Alas, whoever's wedding it was, it did not happen.

I was intrigued by Old Bernard's notion that a wedding was to have taken place after the ill-fated performance. Before I left his magical cavern I asked him if he could find out for me the identity of the bride and groom, for, surely, this must have been a theatrical wedding.

That third night of our run, as anyone connected with the English stage will tell you, was a night of theatrical disaster. Even the most accursed productions of *The Scottish Play* have been accomplished with less misadventure.

Kwame, who had been auditioning in the West End, arrived late to the production, pleading the late running of the seventeen eleven from Charing Cross. He readied himself with such haste that, inevitably, he forgot to don his cricket pads. And, as everybody knows, when I kicked him ferociously in the shins in Act One he was unprotected, and lay groaning on the stage for a good three minutes during which time I extemporised another thrashing episode with my cane. This time I accidentally missed his hunchback cushion and landed my cane full on his bald skull, eliciting gasps of disapproval from an overly sensitive audience. Someone even shouted "shame". Then the heckling began in earnest. Kwame had to be removed from the stage, hyperventilating fussily, while his understudy was ushered in stage left.

And then, Renata, who had been looking even more sullen than usual, managed, during her first encounter with a rather squeaky-voice Prince Ferdinand to fall off the front of the stage completely. (Later she claimed in an American newspaper that she had been pushed by the ghost of Dame Cecelia Raven, if you please). Of course, we professional actors always adopt the attitude that, come what may, *the show must go on*. Petronella and I just acted on regardless but, presently, our speech was drowned out by the screams and Texan oaths projected from beneath the stage.

An audience member stepped forward saying, *I'm a doctor*. Having cursorily examined the supine Renata he announced to a shocked audience that that she had broken both legs and should be conveyed to a hospital post-haste. I do confess that, even then, I just launched into my speech – *If I have too austerely punished you* – regardless; and I was still acting when, for the first time in my career, the curtain fell in mid-act. Apparently, health and safety regulations require the suspension of a performance if a risk of injury is deemed severe. Though, I must say that I was once in a production of *The Mikado* at the *Winter*

Gardens, Blackpool, when the cast continued even though the theatre had actually caught fire. The younger generation, it seems, do not share the reticence of mine.

As I walked off the stage, still hearing the hubbub of a disgruntled and alarmed audience from the other side of the curtain, I glimpsed Adrian eyeing me with a kind of paternal concern.

I then went straight to my dressing room. The corridor had an air of desolation: I had no idea to where the cast had fled. Later, Petronella told me that the entire cast had decamped to the *Wat Tyler* pub, where they proceeded to become, as people who worry about their future often do, raucously drunk.

I sat before the dressing mirror, the very one that had first revealed the face of Sir Adrian Bates. The phone rang. I picked up the receiver and heard Old Bernard's voice. *Mr Bennery on line two for you, Mr Aubrey*. What followed was the most shocking tirade of theatrical venom that I have ever heard, liberally laced with language that would surely make a Neapolitan fishwife blush. Lester was accusing me of having put two of his most promising protégées in hospital. He said there would be court cases and claims for compensation for years; that I had reduced his *oeuvre* to ridicule; and that there was no possibility of recasting. The production would have to close.

I listened, said nothing, and hung up while Lester was in full flow. We never spoke again. I wished that I had told him earlier that I found his entire production concept misguided, but I had taken his shilling. I poured myself a large gin from Oscar's Lalique decanter and added some angostura bitters. I sipped; and then I began to remove my make-up.

At that moment there was a gentle tap upon the door, which by its solicitous rhythm, I reckoned to be Bernard's. I bid Bernard enter. Of course I had supposed that Bernard might come on business related to the disaster that had just occurred. But I was wrong; his purpose was of quite another nature.

My dear Mr Aubrey, he said, *when we met earlier today, I am afraid that I did not reveal to you all that I know, and have carried with me for so many years, about that fateful day when the Priory Theatre was destroyed by a German doodlebug. My relationship with Mr Lennox – Bunny – you see was very close indeed. Well before he passed away he asked me to curate his voluminous correspondence with all the theatrical luminaries of his times. When I pass on, Mr Aubrey, I have left instructions that some twenty four boxes of documents be donated to the British Library.*

That is all perfectly fascinating my dear Bernard, but how does it concern me?

Mr Aubrey, this evening I have removed one document from the archive which was entrusted to me. I hope that dear old Bunny will not scold me when we are finally reunited in the theatre of Heaven. Here it is, Sir.

He placed an antique manila envelope on my dressing table, turned and left the room. I gulped a slug of bitter gin and then picked up the envelope. I knew that copperplate handwriting: for Heaven's sake, it was Larry's. I prized the letter from the envelope and began to read.

Saturday, 19 August 1944
Oh my God, Bunny, what a bloody business.

I was there in Dartford today. Not in your beloved Priory Theatre (though I popped in earlier to see poor Adders). I was at the Church, Holy Trinity just next door with that sweet lovely girl, Hermione Simpkins. Hermione, though heavily pregnant with Adrian's child, radiated the cherubic happiness of the perfect bride to be. You see, Adrian was to have married Hermione today after the matinee...What happened is just too, too cruel...

I agreed to be Adder's secret best man. The plan was to make an honest girl of dear Hermione and to reveal the match later. (Cessy, of course, found out and was livid). Despite the age difference they were head over heels in love. Adders said that when this wretched war is over, he would take her for a proper honeymoon in Venice and then to the Riviera. They even wanted me to come with them.

Two of our brightest stars have been torn out of the sky. And that poor sweet girl is broken, Bunny. The only thing that I can do for dearest Adders now is to support his child who will be born soon to a luckless mother...

As I walked back through the night to the Bull Hotel, I now understood why Larry had always taken such a fatherly interest in my progress; why Mother had become the woman she became; why she never loved me as I might have wished; and how my acting heritage was even more distinguished than I had imagined. But I reflected that we are all singularly ill equipped to judge our parents who have come before us. My Mother, and her endless litany of inappropriate though sometimes moneyed lovers; the embarrassment she caused me at public school by arriving in a taxi unannounced to argue with the Bursar about my fees; her increasingly disastrous run of West End flops; and her inextinguishable will to remain alive. Of course she never married; for she was always married to her indelible grief. And for the first time since early childhood, I felt that I loved her.

Mrs Plender greeted me with uncharacteristic brusqueness. She told me that Lester's people had already cancelled my account.

There was, inevitably, a last blast from the wretched man Snipe who chortled with alacrity at our production's close in the unwholesome *Daily Mail*. *Aubrey Simpkins is out of work again...*

As I waited upon the platform of Dartford Station for the ten thirty five to Charing Cross (eleven minutes late, of course), the last extraordinary spectral manifestation occurred. I watched transfixed as a ghostly train - I believe it is called a *Pullman* from a more gracious age - drew noiselessly into the station. I was astonished by the elegance of its brown and cream colours and brass door handles – and then I read *Venice-Simplon Express*. I knew not then or now if I was experiencing some kind of hallucination or whether I had accidently travelled to another world. The train drew to a halt and I found myself looking through a window into an elegant dining room where evidently an elaborate meal was being served.

Suddenly, the internal lace curtains were parted by a gloved hand. And, pressing my face close against the window, I could make out the magical passengers. And there was Mother, cheek by jowl with my father Adrian, blissfully happy and much in love, drinking Champagne while still entranced by one another. And then I noticed

Larry, sitting opposite them, in his immaculate Prince of Wales cheque suit, detached, but, as always, conspiring. In a sudden moment Larry swivelled his gaze towards the window and met mine looking in. In a gesture of such subtlety that could only ever have been his, he winked at me, but virtually imperceptibly.

In an instant, the ghostly train propelled itself silently out of the station, bound for Dover and beyond. It disappeared into the ether.

I found myself standing on the edge of the platform staring at the empty tracks. And a sweet voice asked me from somewhere behind *Are you quite alright, Aubrey*? The voice of course was Petronella's. I responded: *I'd feel better if you were travelling with me.* And in a moment we were holding hands.

As my train (not at all ghostly – an ugly lumbering beast emblazoned with CONNEX SOUTH EAST) materialised, Petronella asked me *Where are you headed? Maida Vale*, I replied. *You'd like it there*. And she smiled.

Petronella remained with me – apart from absences on tour and then increasingly for film – for nearly four years, across my late fifties, which I count as amongst the happiest of my life. When we returned to the flat, it felt different. My Mother's restless spirit had been calmed and I sensed a warm glow of motherly approval for my new marriage (as I regarded it). I knew that Mother had found peace at last.

Of course, nothing lasts. Petronella, much younger than I, grew restless and then renewed her acquaintance with Kwame Odinga-Jones on a film set in California. Her letter of valediction was unutterably tender; and it was I who felt sorry for her.

As all of you will know, there was a tragic denouement. Petronella and Kwame perished together, in a manner never quite explained, in a light aircraft – a Cessna, with Kwame at the controls – which plunged into the sea just off LA. In the international furore of media lamentation, I was utterly ignored.

Sometimes, in my flat, I will re-enter a room and feel that Mother has just left it. It is as if the cushions of the sofa are still warned by her body heat. And at other times I approach the bathroom door and I can hear Petronella humming and splashing softly, as she always did when her naked body was immersed in luxuriant foam.

I have never been back to Dartford. But once I asked an old theatre hand who had business there to update me on the Priory Theatre and to deliver a small gift to Old Bernard. When I saw the hand again, he told me that not only could he not find the theatre, but everyone he asked denied that it had ever existed. Though for me, it was the place that opened my eyes. I shall never forget it until *all my charms are o'erthrown*.

For what I learnt there is that the dead never leave us, and will always roam amongst us if only we have eyes to see them. That is the nature of this world. And, no doubt, when we ourselves are done, actors or not, we shall be condemned to play for eternity in this theatre of ghosts.

Bite-Sized Books Catalogue

Business Books

Paul Davies
>Developing a Business Plan
>>Making a Persuasive Plan for Your Business

Paul Davies
>Contract Management for Non-Specialists

Paul Davies
>Developing Personal Effectiveness in Business

Paul Davies
>A More Effective Sales Team
>>Sales Management Focused on Sales People

Paul Davies
>The Naked Human in Business
>>Accelerate Your Personal Effectiveness by Understanding Humans – The Practical One Two Three of Business Development

Tim Emmett
>Bid for Success
>>Building the Right Strategy and Team

Nigel Greenwood
>Why You Should Welcome Customer Complaints
>>And What to Do About Them

Nigel Greenwood
>Six Things that All Customer Want
>>A Practical Guide to Delivering Simply Brilliant Customer Service

Stuart Haining
>The Practical Digital Marketeer – Volume 1
>>Digital Marketing – Is It Worth It and Your First Steps

Stuart Haining
>The Practical Digital Marketeer – Volume 2
>>Planning for Success

Lifestyle Books

Phil Davies
    Don't Worry Be Happy
        A Personal Journey
Phil Davies
    Feel the Fear and Pack Anyway
        Around the World in 284 Days
Stuart Haining
    My Other Car is an Aston
        A Practical Guide to Ownership and Other
        Excuses to Quit Work and Start a Business
Stuart Haining
    After the Supercar
        You've Got the Dream Car – But Is It Easy
        to Part With?
Bill Heine
    Cancer
        Living Behind Enemy Lines Without a Map
Regina Kerschbaumer
    Yoga Coffee and a Glass of Wine
        A Yoga Journey
Gillian Perry
    Capturing the Celestial Lights
        A Practical Guide to Imagining the
        Northern Lights
Arthur Worrell
    A Grandfather's Story
        Arthur Worrell's War

Public Affairs Books

David Bailey, John Mair and Neil Fowler (Editors)
    Keeping the Wheels on the Road – Brexit Book 3
        UK Auto Post Brexit

Eben Black
        Lies Lobbying and Lunch
                PR, Public Affairs and Political
                Engagement – A Guide
Paul Davies, John Mair and Neil Fowler
        Will the Tory Party Ever Be the Same? – Brexit
        Book 4
                The Effect of Brexit
John Mair and Neil Fowler (Editors)
        Oil Dorado
                Guyana's Black Gold
John Mair and Richard Keeble (Editors)
        Investigative Journalism Today:
                Speaking Truth to Power
John Mair and Neil Fowler (Editors)
        Do They Mean Us – Brexit Book 1
                The Foreign Correspondents' View of the
                British Brexit
John Mair, Alex De Ruyter and Neil Fowler (Editors)
        The Case for Brexit – Brexit Book 2
John Mair, Richard Keeble and Farrukh Dhondy (Editors)
        V.S Naipaul:
                The legacy
John Mills
        Economic Growth Post Brexit
                How the UK Should Take on the World
Christian Wolmar
        Wolmar for London
                Creating a Grassroots Campaign in a
                Digital Age

Fiction

Paul Davies
> The Ways We Live Now
>> Civil Service Corruption, Wilful Blindness, Commercial Fraud, and Personal Greed – a Novel of Our Times

Paul Davies
> Coming To
>> A Novel of Self-Realisation

Children's Books

Chris Reeve – illustrations by Mike Tingle
> The Dictionary Boy
>> A Salutary Tale

Fredrik Payedar
> The Spirit of Chaos
>> It Begins

Printed in Great Britain
by Amazon